Flickering

MICHAEL MANOSCA

EDITED BY
REGENA SLATER

For that young man I met at a holiday party in 1996, and for all of us who learned that family is something you choose.

"And here I have lamely related to you the uneventful chronicle of two foolish children in a flat who most unwisely sacrificed for each other the greatest treasures of their house. But in a last word to the wise of these days let it be said that of all who give gifts these two were the wisest."

"THE GIFT OF THE MAGI" O. HENRY

Preface

Many years ago, I walked among the crowd as one of three hosts at a Halloween party my roommates and I were throwing. Many people stuffed our modest rented home on the edge of Old Louisville, word having spread among friends of friends. It was a costume party, so I was enjoying guessing who I knew and who lay beneath each mask.

Walking into our upstairs family room, I found someone sitting alone, staring around in quiet awe at the genial chaos of the evening, as if needing a breather. Poor kid, I thought. He looked like someone had thrown him in the deep end and walked away, and I knew the feeling. I always had to give myself a pep talk when we held these festivities—crowds weren't my thing.

We had the most delightful conversation amidst strangers and friends walking through, cocktails and costumes, music and dancing—the whole joyful mess. He was newly out and this was his first "real gathering" with "real gay people." I smiled. I wasn't that much older, but I still wrestled with how to feel comfortable in my own skin.

We went on to share our stories, enjoy each other's company, and laugh at the impromptu costume contest my roommate began. There was something easy about being around each other, something my instincts told me he probably needed. I got a Christmas card from him that year—back when people used to do that sort of thing—and often wondered whatever happened to him every holiday season since.

I suppose we were both living our lives, but somehow the holiday season—which for us gay folk begins on Halloween and culminates with New Year's Day hangovers—reminds me of that young man, and of me as a young man as well.

My first attempt at a holiday story could include no other inspiration than him. In a season where we were all practically forced to have a holly jolly everything, our ragtag community of misfits—most having been thrown away by their families, many suffering losses unimaginable to those who spoke in dismissive tones during the AIDS crisis—had little to celebrate other than the love we gave each other, often at our own expense.

This holiday story, I hope, shares some of those feelings: both delight and fear, joy in the love that is simple and caring, and the hope that while many celebrate a season of merriment, those of us who carry a sleigh full of complex emotions can find our own quiet miracles along the way.

One

In winter's fiercest hour,
when all doors should close,
the lost discover
they were never truly
alone.

CALLUM CAMPBELL STOOD in the doorway of David Morrison's living room, watching his friends navigate the careful choreography of his first Christmas without Evan. They moved around him like dancers who'd rehearsed their steps— never lingering too long in conversation, never letting silence stretch into something that might invite unwanted memories, never quite meeting his eyes when they mentioned holiday plans or New Year's resolutions.

"More eggnog, Callum?" David appeared at his elbow with a crystal tumbler, the rich cream mixture garnished with fresh nutmeg. Everything about David's holiday gathering was perfect, from the precisely arranged garland draped along the mantelpiece to the tasteful jazz trio playing softly in the corner. No detail had been overlooked in what Callum recognized as a collective effort to create the perfect distraction.

"I'm fine, thanks." Callum raised his half-full glass, forcing what he hoped passed for a grateful smile. Through the bay windows, he could see snow beginning to fall in fat, lazy flakes that caught the light from the street lamps. The weather forecast had called for a light dusting, nothing more.

"Callum." Michael Wright materialized beside David, both men flanking him now with the practiced ease of concerned friends. "Janet was just asking about your book project. That research you've been working on?"

There it was—the lifeline they'd collectively decided to throw him. The mysterious academic project that justified his absence from their gatherings over the past months, that explained why he no longer joined them for dinner parties or weekend trips to the mountains. Callum had mentioned it once, offhandedly, when someone had pressed too hard about how he was spending his time, and now it had taken on a life of its own.

"It's coming along," he said, the lie sliding out as smoothly as it had dozens of times before. "Still in the research phase, you know how it is."

David nodded knowingly, though Callum suspected he knew exactly what he was doing. They all did, probably. They were all too intelligent, too perceptive, to believe that Callum Campbell had suddenly become a hermit scholar. But they played along because it was easier than acknowledging what everyone in the room understood: that their friend was barely holding himself together, and had been since March.

"Well, when you're ready to share it with us..." Michael let the sentence hang, diplomatic and warm.

Callum nodded and moved toward the windows, ostensibly

vid's holiday decorations but really to put some
between himself and their kindness. It was suffocating,
this careful attention. He understood it came from love—
these men had been his and Evan's closest friends for years, had
been their chosen family when blood family wouldn't suffice.
They'd been the ones to quietly handle arrangements when Evan
died, to field phone calls and grocery shop and sit with Callum
during those first terrible weeks when getting out of bed felt
impossible.

But understanding their motives didn't make it easier to
breathe.

Outside, the snow was falling harder now, coating the sidewalks with a thin layer of white. Through the window, he could
see other houses along Cherokee Road, their windows glowing
warmly, families presumably gathered inside for their own
holiday celebrations. Normal families, with normal grief and
normal joy and normal problems that didn't require this level of
choreographed careful handling.

"Callum?"

He turned to find Elena Rodriguez approaching with a plate
of David's famous pecan tartlets. Elena taught Spanish literature
at U of L, and she'd been the one to organize tonight's gathering,
though she'd been careful to make it seem like David's idea.

"You seem a million miles away," she said gently.

"Just watching the snow," he replied. "It's getting heavier."

Elena glanced toward the window, her face brightening. "Can
you believe it? They're saying we might get six to eight inches
now. A real white Christmas for once! Won't that be wonderful?"

The thought of being trapped here overnight, of enduring
breakfast and more careful conversation and another day of
being handled like something fragile, made Callum's chest
tighten.

"I should probably head home before it gets worse," he said.

"Oh, Cal, don't be silly. It's not that bad yet, and we haven't even had dinner." The words were out before Elena could stop them, and Callum felt the familiar stab of pain that came every time someone used Evan's nickname for him. Around them, conversation seemed to pause for just a moment—not long enough for anyone else to notice, but long enough for the handful of people who knew to feel the weight of the mistake.

Elena's face went pale. Across the room, David's eyes found hers with a sharp, concerned look that said everything: *How could you forget? We've all been so careful.*

"I mean, Callum," she corrected quickly, her voice carrying just a hint of the concern they were all working so hard to disguise. "Besides, David went to so much trouble..."

But the damage was done. Only one person had ever been allowed to call him Cal, and that person had been dead for nine months.

He looked around the room again—at David adjusting the lighting, at Michael ensuring everyone had drinks, at Janet and Robert deep in animated conversation with two other couples, all of them stealing glances his way when they thought he wasn't looking. They meant well. They loved him. And he was going to disappoint them by leaving early, just as he'd disappointed them by declining their Thanksgiving invitation, their suggestions for weekend trips, their carefully casual invitations to movies and dinners and all the small social rituals that were supposed to help him heal.

"I really should go," he said, setting his barely touched eggnog on a side table. "I've got papers to grade this weekend, and with the weather..."

It was another lie. He'd finished grading his students' final papers days ago, had turned in his grades and officially begun his winter break. But Elena nodded as if she believed him, or as if she understood that he needed her to believe him.

"Of course," she said quietly, the shame of her slip still coloring her voice. "Drive carefully, won't you? And call when you get home?"

"I will."

The ritual of goodbyes took another ten minutes—handshakes and embraces, promises to call soon, invitations for New Year's Eve that they all knew he wouldn't accept. David pressed a container of leftover tartlets into his hands, and Janet made him promise to take care of himself. They clustered around him at the front door, watching as he pulled on his winter coat and wound his scarf around his neck.

"Merry Christmas, Callum," David said, and there was something in his voice that suggested he knew this evening hadn't achieved what they'd all hoped it would.

"Merry Christmas," Callum replied, and stepped out into the falling snow.

The cold hit him immediately, sharp and clean after the warm, careful atmosphere inside. Snow swirled around the streetlights, and he could already see that his car would need to be brushed off. The weather really was getting worse—Elena had been right about that, even if her optimism about a "wonderful" white Christmas felt like something from another person's life.

He fumbled with his keys, his hands already stiff from the cold, and started the engine to let it warm while he cleared the windshield. The snow was heavier than it looked, packed and icy where it had started to accumulate. By the time he'd scraped the windows clean, his shoulders were covered with fresh powder.

Callum pulled away from the curb slowly, feeling the tires slip slightly before finding purchase. Cherokee Road was normally a busy thoroughfare, but tonight it was nearly empty—most people had the sense to stay home in weather like this. The few cars he did see were creeping along like he was, their headlights cutting weak cones through the swirling snow.

He should have stayed. That was the rational thing to do, the considerate thing. David's house was warm and safe, and his friends genuinely wanted him there. But the thought of another few hours of their careful attention, of pretending that their determined cheerfulness was helping instead of highlighting exactly how broken he still was, felt impossible.

At the intersection of Cherokee and Bardstown Road, his car slid slightly as he braked for the red light. The storm was definitely worsening—the snow was falling so heavily now that his wipers could barely keep up. Through the passenger window, he could see the lights of the shops and restaurants along Bardstown Road, most of them still open despite the weather. People hurried along the sidewalks with their heads down, clutching shopping bags and pulling their coats tight.

Normal people, living normal lives, dealing with normal winter weather instead of the kind of internal storm that made even the simplest social interactions feel like drowning.

The light changed, and he turned onto Bardstown Road, heading toward the Watterson Expressway that would take him home to Old Louisville. But as he accelerated, he felt the back end of the car slide out slightly. His hands tightened on the steering wheel, and he eased off the gas, feeling his heart rate spike.

He was a careful driver normally, had been since his teenage years in Owensboro when his younger brother had wrapped his pickup truck around a tree during an ice storm. But careful driving required focus, and focus had been in short supply since March. His mind kept drifting—to Elena's slip of the tongue, to the way David's eyes had gone sharp with concern, to how much he missed hearing someone call him Cal in a voice full of love instead of accidental pain.

By the time he reached the on-ramp for I-264, the snow was coming down so hard that he could barely see the taillights of the car ahead of him. His windshield wipers were struggling, leaving smeared arcs of visibility that cleared for only seconds before being obscured again. The smart thing would be to pull off, find a restaurant or gas station, wait for the worst of it to pass.

But the thought of sitting in some brightly lit place, surrounded by strangers who were probably calling their families to let them know they were safe, felt almost as unbearable as staying at David's party had been. At least in his car, he could be alone with his grief without having to perform normalcy for anyone else.

The expressway was treacherous—he could see where other cars had slid off the road, their hazard lights blinking through the snow like distress signals. Callum gripped the steering wheel tighter and focused on the faint red glow of taillights ahead of him, using them as a guide through the white chaos.

He was thinking about Evan—about how Evan would have insisted they stay at David's, would have made him hot chocolate when they finally got home and teased him about being antisocial. Evan had always been better at accepting care from their friends, better at letting people help without feeling like he was disappointing them somehow. Cal, Evan would have said, they love you. Let them.

But Evan wasn't there to say it, and the absence felt as sharp as the wind cutting through the gaps in his car windows.

The exit for Old Louisville appeared through the snow like a gift, and Callum carefully maneuvered down the ramp, feeling his tires struggle for traction on the slick surface. At the bottom of the ramp, instead of turning right toward his house on St. James Court, he found himself turning left, toward the commercial strip that lined this edge of downtown.

He wasn't sure why—maybe he wasn't ready to go home to his empty house and the guest room that still made his chest ache every time he walked past it. Maybe he just wanted to drive a little longer, to stay suspended in this white cocoon where he didn't have to think about Christmas morning or the stack of holiday cards on his kitchen counter that he couldn't bring himself to open.

That's when he saw the Wendy's sign through the snow, its red and yellow glow barely visible through the storm. And that's when his car hit a patch of ice on the street, sending him sliding sideways across the empty parking lot toward the restaurant's front windows.

The car spun in what felt like slow motion, his headlights sweeping across the snow-covered asphalt before coming to rest just a few feet from a light pole. Callum sat there for a moment, his heart hammering, hands still gripping the steering wheel. The engine was still running, the heater still blowing warm air, but he could feel his whole body shaking—whether from the near accident or something deeper, he wasn't sure.

He could have died. The thought hit him with surprising clarity. If he'd been going faster, if the light pole hadn't been there to stop him, if he'd slid into traffic instead of an empty parking lot. He could have died, and the strangest part was that for just a moment, sitting there in his car with snow pelting the windshield, he wasn't sure how he felt about that.

Through the passenger window, he could see the Wendy's restaurant, its windows glowing warmly against the storm. There was a car parked around back—probably an employee working late. The front entrance was only about twenty feet away, close enough that he could make it without getting completely soaked.

He could reverse, try to make it home, hope that the roads weren't too bad and that he could navigate the rest of the drive without another accident. Or he could sit here until the storm passed, running his engine and hoping he didn't run out of gas.

Or he could go inside.

The thought surprised him. He didn't eat fast food, hadn't

been in a place like this in years. But the warm light spilling out onto the snow looked inviting in a way that his empty house didn't, and the idea of human contact—even the minimal interaction with a cashier taking his order—felt suddenly appealing after the suffocating care of his friends and the isolation of his drive.

Before he could change his mind, Callum turned off the engine and pulled his coat tighter around him. The cold hit him like a physical blow when he opened the car door, and by the time he reached the restaurant entrance, his shoulders were covered with snow and his cheeks stung from the wind.

He hoped it wasn't too late—he had no idea what time places like this closed, especially during a storm. But when he pulled on the door handle, it gave way easily, opening with a blast of warm air and the soft chime of entrance bells.

Callum stepped inside, brushing snow from his coat and stomping his feet on the entry mat. The restaurant was empty except for the soft sounds coming from behind the counter—someone moving around in the kitchen area, the distant sound of water running.

"Hello?" he called out, his voice echoing slightly in the empty dining room. "Are you still open?"

There was a crash from the kitchen—something metal hitting the floor—followed by a muffled curse. Then footsteps, quick and nervous, and a young man appeared from behind the counter.

He was tall and slim, maybe nineteen or twenty, with dark wavy hair that looked like it needed a trim. He wore the standard Wendy's uniform—burgundy polo shirt and dark pants—but even the generic work clothes couldn't hide his striking features: sharp cheekbones, full lips, the kind of face that belonged in a magazine. What caught Callum's attention, though, were his eyes, which held a wariness that seemed too old for someone his age, and the way his uniform looked wrinkled and slept-in despite his otherwise careful appearance.

When he saw Callum, those eyes went wide with something that looked like panic.

"I..." the young man started, then stopped, looking toward the door as if calculating whether he could make it past Callum and outside. "We're... I mean, I was just..."

And Callum realized, with a clarity that cut through his own grief and confusion, that this young man was afraid. Not just startled by an unexpected customer, but genuinely, deeply afraid.

"I'm sorry," Callum said gently, keeping his voice low and non-threatening. "I didn't mean to scare you. I just... my car slid on the ice outside, and I saw your lights were on. I thought maybe I could wait here until the storm lets up a little."

The young man looked toward the windows, where snow was still falling heavily, then back at Callum. His hands were shaking slightly, and Callum noticed that his fingernails were clean and manicured—an odd detail that seemed at odds with his obvious distress.

"We're... we're supposed to be closed," the young man said, but there was no conviction in his voice. "I was just... cleaning up."

"Of course," Callum said. "I can go if you need me to. I just thought..." He gestured toward the storm outside. "It's pretty bad out there."

And in that moment, looking at this frightened young man who was clearly alone and clearly struggling with something much bigger than an unexpected customer, Callum forgot about his own pain for the first time in months.

Two

*When you have
nothing left,
every sound
becomes a threat,
every shadow a reminder of
how far
you've fallen.*

JAMES MCCARTHY HAD BEEN SCRUBBING the same section of the grill for the past twenty minutes, not because it needed it, but because the repetitive motion kept his hands busy and his mind from spiraling into the panic that had been building all evening. The restaurant had been closed for two hours, but he'd volunteered to stay and finish the cleaning—partly because Dan, his manager, had seemed relieved to have someone willing to work late during the storm, and partly because James had nowhere else to go.

The cardboard he'd hidden behind the stack of Pepsi syrup boxes was still there, along with the thin blanket he'd stolen from the lost and found. It wasn't much, but it was shelter, and after six weeks of this routine, James had learned to be grateful for small mercies.

He'd almost been caught that morning. Dan had come in early to check on the building's heating system and had found James emerging from the storage room, hair disheveled, trying to smooth out his uniform shirt. James had quickly invented a story about coming in early to get a head start on prep work, but Dan's eyes had lingered on him with suspicion that made James's stomach clench.

"Just make sure you're not here when I open tomorrow morning," Dan had said quietly, and James had nodded, understanding the warning. One more slip-up and he'd be out of a job —and out of the only warm place he had to sleep.

The metal pot crashed to the floor with a sound that echoed through the empty restaurant, jolting James from his thoughts. His hands were shaking more than usual tonight, probably from the cold that seemed to seep through the building's walls despite the heating system running constantly. Or maybe it was hunger—he'd eaten nothing but a small bag of chips since this morning, rationing what little money he had left.

The irony wasn't lost on him that he was starving while surrounded by food. He could have easily made himself a burger or grabbed some fries, but the security cameras mounted in every corner of the kitchen made that impossible. Even if there hadn't been cameras watching his every move, James knew he wouldn't have been able to bring himself to steal. It was the last shred of dignity he had left—the final line he refused to cross. He'd lost his family, his home, his future, but he wouldn't become a thief. Not yet.

He bent to retrieve the pot, cursing under his breath, when he heard the voice from the dining room.

"Hello? Are you still open?"

James froze, the pot clutched in his hands. The front door was supposed to be locked—he was sure he'd locked it when Dan left at eight. But the voice was real, and it was coming from someone who was definitely inside the restaurant.

His mind raced through possibilities: a robber, someone looking for drugs or money from the register, or worse—someone who knew he was sleeping here and had come to report him. The police would be called, and then what? He'd be arrested for trespassing, and even if they didn't charge him, they'd call his parents. He could already picture his father's face when he got that call.

"We're... I mean, I was just..." James called out, emerging from the kitchen area. His voice cracked slightly, betraying his fear, and he cleared his throat, trying to sound more confident than he felt.

The man standing by the entrance was nothing like what James had expected. He was older, maybe mid-thirties, with a short beard and kind eyes that seemed tired in a way that went deeper than physical exhaustion. His winter coat was expensive-looking but not flashy, and snow clung to his shoulders and hair. He looked like someone's father, or maybe a professor—the kind of person who would normally have no reason to be in a place like this.

But it was the man's expression that caught James off guard. Instead of anger or suspicion or even annoyance at finding the restaurant technically closed, there was something that looked almost like concern. The man was looking at James as if he could see right through his carefully constructed facade, and James felt suddenly, acutely aware of how he must appear: young, scared, obviously out of place.

"I'm sorry," the man said, and his voice was gentle, almost apologetic. "I didn't mean to scare you. I just... my car slid on the ice outside, and I saw your lights were on. I thought maybe I could wait here until the storm lets up a little."

James looked past the man toward the windows, where snow was falling so heavily it was almost impossible to see the parking lot. The storm had been building all evening, and the weather reports had started talking about record snowfall, the kind of blizzard that shut down entire cities. Even if he wanted to kick this man out, it would be cruel to send him back into that weather.

But letting him stay meant conversation, meant pretending to be a normal employee working a normal late shift, when the truth was that James was barely holding himself together. His hands were still shaking, and he could feel sweat gathering at the back of his neck despite the cold.

"We're... we're supposed to be closed," James said, hating how uncertain he sounded. He was nineteen years old, had been student body vice president at St. X, had given speeches in front of hundreds of people. But standing here in his wrinkled uniform, looking at this stranger who seemed to see too much, he felt like a child playing dress-up in an adult's world.

"Of course," the man said. "I can go if you need me to. I just thought..." He gestured toward the storm outside. "It's pretty bad out there."

And there it was—the kindness James had been avoiding for weeks, the simple human decency that he'd learned to be suspicious of because it usually came with questions he couldn't answer. Why was he working so late? Where did he live? Did his parents know he was here? Questions that would unravel the thin story he'd constructed around his survival.

But this man wasn't asking questions. He was just standing there, snow melting on his coat, waiting for James to make a deci-

Three

When winter winds blow
harsh and deep,
and strangers meet
where secrets sleep,
the first small words we dare to share
might lift the weight
we've learned to bear.

CALLUM BRUSHED the remaining snow from his coat and looked around the empty restaurant, taking in details that spoke of a place winding down for the night. The chairs were already stacked on most of the tables, the floors gleamed with fresh mopping, and the air carried the lingering smell of industrial cleaner mixed with the faint aroma of fryer oil. Everything suggested a conscientious employee finishing up his shift—except for the young man standing behind the counter, whose hands were still shaking slightly and whose eyes kept darting toward the door as if he expected someone else to walk in at any moment.

"I really appreciate this," Callum said, settling into one of the few booths that still had its chairs down. The vinyl seat was cold against his back, but the simple act of sitting somewhere warm and dry felt like a luxury after the harrowing drive through the storm. "I wasn't sure I was going to make it home in one piece."

James nodded but didn't respond immediately. Instead, he busied himself wiping down a counter that already looked spotless, his movements quick and nervous. Callum watched him work, noting the way the young man's uniform hung slightly loose on his frame, as if he'd lost weight recently, and how his dark hair fell across his forehead in a way that made him look even younger than he probably was.

"Have you been working here long?" Callum asked, trying for casual conversation that might put the young man at ease.

"A few months," James replied without looking up from his cleaning. His voice was carefully neutral, the kind of practiced tone people used when they didn't want to reveal anything about themselves.

Callum recognized the deflection—he'd been using similar tactics himself for nine months, steering conversations away from anything personal, anything that might lead to questions about Evan or explanations about why he spent his evenings alone instead of building the kind of social life expected of a man his age. But where Callum's evasions came from grief, this young man's seemed to stem from something closer to fear.

"I'm sorry about barging in like this," Callum said. "I know you were probably looking forward to getting home."

Something flickered across James's face—too quick to read, but it looked almost like panic. "It's fine," he said quickly. "I wasn't... I mean, the storm's pretty bad. You shouldn't be driving in it."

There was something in the way he said it that caught Callum's attention. Not the words themselves, but the slight hesitation before them, as if James had been about to say something else entirely. The kind of slip that suggested whatever story this young man was telling about his life, it wasn't the complete truth.

Callum knew something about incomplete truths.

Outside, the wind howled around the building, rattling the windows and sending snow spiraling past the glass in hypnotic patterns. The storm seemed to be getting worse by the minute, but without a radio or television, it was impossible to know just how bad it might become. The weather forecast that morning had called for light snow—nothing like this.

"I had no idea it was going to be this bad," Callum said, watching the snow pile against the windows. "The forecast said a dusting at most."

"Same here," James agreed. "Dan—my manager—he would've made us close early if he'd known. This is..." He gestured toward the windows. "This is something else."

Callum frowned, thinking about Elena and the others back at David's party. "I was supposed to call when I got home," he said, more to himself than to James. "Let people know I made it safely."

"Your wife?" James asked, then immediately looked like he regretted the question.

"No," Callum said, and felt the familiar tightness in his chest that came whenever he had to navigate questions about his personal life. "A friend. She gets anxious during storms."

It wasn't entirely a lie. Elena would worry if she didn't hear from him, though probably more about his emotional state than his physical safety. But it was easier than trying to explain the complicated dynamics of his chosen family, or the way grief had made him feel responsible for everyone else's peace of mind while simultaneously pushing them all away.

James nodded and went back to his cleaning, but Callum noticed the way his shoulders had relaxed slightly at the mention of a concerned friend. As if the idea of someone caring enough to worry was something he understood, or maybe something he missed.

"What about you?" Callum asked. "Anyone expecting you home tonight?"

The question was innocent enough—the kind of small talk people made when trapped together by bad weather. But James's reaction was immediate and unmistakable: his whole body went rigid, his hands stilled on the counter, and for a moment he looked like he might bolt for the door despite the storm raging outside.

"I..." James started, then stopped. His knuckles were white where he gripped the cleaning rag. "No. No one's expecting me."

The words came out flat and final, but underneath them Callum heard something that sounded like grief. Not the sharp, fresh grief of recent loss, but the deeper ache of absence that had been carved hollow by time and circumstances. It was a tone he recognized because he'd heard it in his own voice for months.

"I'm sorry," Callum said gently. "I didn't mean to pry."

James looked up then, meeting Callum's eyes for the first time since they'd exchanged names. "You weren't. It's just..." He trailed off, then seemed to make a decision. "It's complicated."

Callum nodded. "Complicated" was a word he'd been using a lot lately himself. It was what he told colleagues when they asked about his weekend plans, what he told his brother when he called from Owensboro wondering why Callum hadn't been home for a visit. It was a perfectly useful word that acknowledged the existence of a story without actually telling it.

"I understand complicated," he said.

Something in his tone must have conveyed that he meant it, because James set down his cleaning rag and really looked at him. Not the quick, nervous glances he'd been stealing since Callum walked in, but a genuine appraisal, as if he were trying to figure out whether this stranger could be trusted with even the smallest piece of truth.

"Can I ask you something?" James said finally.

"Sure."

"What were you doing out in this storm? I mean, nobody drives in weather like this unless they have to."

It was Callum's turn to hesitate. The honest answer was that he'd been running from his friends' kindness, from their determined efforts to help him heal, from the suffocating weight of their love and his inability to accept it. But that explanation would require talking about Evan, about loss, about the way grief could make you feel like a stranger in your own life.

"I was at a party," he said instead. "A Christmas party. It was... too much."

James nodded slowly, as if he understood exactly what "too much" meant in this context. "The holidays are hard," he said quietly.

"Yes," Callum agreed. "They are."

They sat in comfortable silence for a moment, the only sounds the storm outside and the gentle hum of the restaurant's heating system. It wasn't much—two strangers sharing the most basic acknowledgment of seasonal sadness—but it felt like the first honest exchange either of them had had in a long time.

"I could make some coffee," James offered suddenly. "If you want. The machine's still on."

Callum looked at this young man who was clearly struggling with his own demons, offering what little comfort he could provide, and felt something shift in his chest. It had been months since anyone had offered to take care of him in such a simple, uncomplicated way—no agenda, no underlying worry about his emotional state, just the basic kindness of hot coffee on a cold night.

"That would be nice," he said. "Thank you."

James moved behind the counter with more confidence than he'd shown before, his hands steady as he worked the coffee machine. Whatever walls he'd built around himself were still firmly in place, but for this moment at least, he seemed willing to let Callum stay on his side of them.

And for the first time since March, Callum found himself genuinely curious about another person's story.

Four

The heart that bears its grief alone
will crack beneath
the weight it's grown,
and tears held back through countless nights
will fall like snow
in winter's blight.

THE WIND HOWLED OUTSIDE and Callum adjusted his coat, caught between being too hot bundled up in the booth and feeling the cold seep through the window beside his shoulder. He caught sight of James struggling with the coffee maker—obviously not a devotee of the world's most sanctioned drug—and let his eyes wander around the room.

It was typical fast food décor, but it looked like it had seen better days, the owner stretching the tired furnishings and worn furniture well beyond their shelf life. Over by the door, just before the hallway leading to the restrooms with their industrial locks (to deter the homeless from using them for public bathing, Callum guessed), sat a pathetic excuse for a Christmas tree. It was still lit with a single strand of lights thrown on haphazardly, probably an assignment given to some hourly worker who didn't give a damn.

The four—no, five—bulbs Callum counted were cheap plastic, looking like they'd seen plenty of Christmases over the years. There wasn't even a star or any kind of topper, nor a skirt on the floor to disguise the obvious trio of green plastic legs anchoring what had to be the least realistic tree Callum had ever seen.

Someone should put it out of its misery, he thought, then paused, shaking his head. *I know exactly how you feel.*

"Uh, here's your coffee."

Callum startled away from his critique of the restaurant's only nod to the holiday season and turned toward James's voice. The young man stood over his booth, holding a steaming mug.

"I... I hope it's okay. I don't really drink coffee." James looked downcast, apologetic. "I'm... uh... sorry. Just..."

"I'm sure it's fine," Callum said, forcing a genial tone. "I appreciate you making it." The more he looked at James, the less he thought about himself.

James turned to walk back to the counter when Callum felt an urgent need to stop him, as if there were an invisible line that, once James crossed it, would prevent them from speaking again. And Callum wanted to speak—he just didn't know about what, or why. Hell, he'd spent all evening conjuring polite excuses to avoid talking. He'd spent the last nine months doing the same thing, if he was honest with himself.

Which, until lately, he hadn't been.

Hadn't been honest about how much this hurt. How much this stupid season squeezed around him like a vise, forcing him to be merry, to forget the past, to sing and laugh and proclaim to the entire world that joy had indeed come to the world. And he couldn't. He couldn't play their game anymore, not when they wouldn't even let him live his real life. His life with Evan. His loss of him.

The endless nights watching Evan struggle to breathe, to hang on. The guilt Callum felt for sometimes wishing it would end—he couldn't watch him slowly suffocate anymore. The countless days teaching his classes, trying to forget what was happening at home, living in *their* world because *their* world didn't give a damn about his. Didn't want to even imagine that he and Evan had existed—that they had been hopelessly in love with each other, dedicated, building a life together while trying to navigate a world where they could be fired, kicked out, or worse...

The breakdown hit without warning. He couldn't do this. Not here. Not in front of this kid.

No. He needed to leave. None of this felt right. He should have just gone home, walked past Evan's old office that he'd forced himself to convert into a guest bedroom just to placate everyone, to show them he was okay, that he'd moved on. He should have crawled into bed and cursed himself for allowing this stupid pity party...

The tears came harder, and he nearly knocked over the coffee cup he hadn't even touched.

Shaking his head as if he could shake away the tears, he began sliding out of the booth. "I'm... sorry. I... I need to go..."

James had felt his feet planted to the grease-filmed tile floor. He'd turned just in front of the closed cash register when he heard the man—what was his name again? Cal-something?—crying. Not just crying, but fighting sobs, heaving in his heavy coat that seemed to swallow him up, still holding the cup of bad coffee James had made, spilling drops across the table.

"Are... are you okay?" James asked hesitantly.

Of course he's not okay, you idiot! he thought, adding to the pile of emotional wreckage he was already drowning under. But he had no idea what to do. Random customers didn't usually come in and break down over bad coffee—at least, he hadn't worked there long enough to know if they did.

Callum had already stood and was pulling out his wallet, mumbling something about how much he owed, but James remained frozen, his legs seemingly disconnected from his brain.

"Listen, uh... sir," James started, worried. He couldn't let this guy—whoever he was—go out into that storm. Hadn't he said something about almost crashing?

"It's... I'm okay," Callum fought to bring himself under control. This was ridiculous, he told himself. He was a grown man—he needed to act like one. He waved off James's concerns the same way he always dismissed people who asked if they could "do anything."

Sure, he always wanted to scream. *Bring back Evan! My precious Evan...*

Again, he fought back a sob. Why was this happening here? He fumbled for his wallet and held out a ten-dollar bill, just wanting James to take it so he could leave.

James's eyes widened—not because of the money, though he could certainly use it, but because he suddenly recognized something in Callum's expression. Something James had been feeling lately, or rather the absence of something: hope. The storm tonight had felt like his last tether to holding onto any himself.

But seeing Callum's face, seeing that same hollow emptiness he'd been carrying—something stirred in James's chest. *I found some more hope for you*, a voice seemed to whisper. *I found it right here. It's not much, but maybe it'll be enough.*

Without conscious thought, James moved. It happened so fast he felt like a passenger in his own body, walking up to Callum and wrapping his arms around him—the kind of embrace he'd been craving since his own world had collapsed.

Callum had been fighting so hard with his internal battle that it took a moment to register what was happening. This boy—really, he was just a kid—the one Callum had recognized as being swallowed by his own dark cloud, was holding him. No one had dared embrace him since Evan had...

Died.

The word hit him like a physical blow. He'd been trying to avoid it. Even when Evan's machines in the hospital—those fucking machines Callum had come to think of as doomsday clocks—had finally gone quiet, even then he couldn't say it. Evan had "passed away," had "gone beyond," had...

But the truth crashed over him now. Evan was dead.

Dead.

And he would never have him back.

Never.

And this kid was holding him the way Evan used to when Callum got worked up and Evan knew he just needed someone to anchor him. But that had been Evan's job.

Evan's.

James held tight, not understanding why, knowing nothing except that he needed to hang on.

And eventually, Callum let him. He held on as if he were falling, because he was. His spirit had finally let go of its careful control. All he wanted for Christmas was Evan.

His precious Evan.

Five

In youth we think that love
will come with trumpets
and fanfare,
but sometimes it arrives
as quiet as a
question.

THE RADIO in the theatre classroom was playing "My Sharona" for what had to be the fourth time that morning, the tinny speakers crackling with static as The Knack's guitar riff echoed off the empty seats. It had been left on from Professor Henderson's prep time earlier, filling the space while students filtered in and settled into their seats.

Callum Campbell shifted his backpack to his other shoulder and checked the course schedule in his hand one more time, making sure he was in the right place.

Theatre 101. Introduction to Theatre Arts. MWF at 10:00 AM.

He still couldn't believe he'd signed up for this. One week into spring semester as a sophomore, and he was scrambling to pick up an elective credit because his advisor had discovered an error in his transcript. Most of the good classes were full, leaving him with choices like "Contemporary Pottery" or "Folk Dancing for Fitness"—neither of which appealed to a farm boy from Owensboro who'd already endured enough ribbing from his dormmates about his thick Kentucky accent and his habit of saying "please" and "thank you" to everyone.

Theatre seemed safer. They were just acting out stories, he figured. Besides, it might be fun to be someone he wasn't for once in his life—maybe someone more confident, more interesting. Someone who didn't spend Saturday nights in his dorm room reading while his roommate went to parties.

The classroom was filling up with students, mostly freshmen by the look of them, settling into their usual seats with the casual familiarity of a class that had been meeting for a week. But Callum could sense their curiosity as he took his seat in the front row—subtle glances his way, wondering who he was and why he'd suddenly appeared in their established group. Callum chose a seat in the front row—a habit from high school that his mother had drilled into him—and pulled out a notebook, trying to look like he belonged.

Professor Henderson swept in five minutes late, a dramatic woman in flowing scarves whose graying hair was still parted down the middle like she'd stepped straight out of 1969. She had a reputation on campus as both the best theatre teacher and the most reliable source for certain extracurricular herbs, though no one ever said so directly. Her claim to fame was having been at Woodstock—she'd mention it at least once every semester, usually while discussing the importance of "authentic emotional expression."

She immediately commanded the room's attention by turning off the radio mid-song and announcing that they would begin each class with breathing exercises. "The breath," she proclaimed, "is the foundation of all performance. I learned that from a shaman I met in a Buffalo commune back in '71."

As students around him began the prescribed deep breathing, Callum found his attention drifting to the empty seat beside him. Most of the other chairs were occupied now, but this one remained vacant, and he wondered if someone had dropped the class or simply overslept.

That's when the door opened and someone slipped in, moving quickly but trying not to cause a disruption. Callum glanced over and felt his breath catch.

The newcomer was small—couldn't be more than five-foot-four—with short brown hair and a face that looked almost impossibly young. He was dressed simply in jeans and a sweatshirt, white socks visible above his black Converse sneakers, but there was something about the way he carried himself that suggested he could handle whatever the world threw at him despite his size.

The young man's eyes swept the room, looking for an available seat, and when they landed on the empty chair next to Callum, he smiled—a quick, infectious grin that made Callum's stomach do something strange.

"Am I late?" the newcomer whispered as he settled into the seat, dumping his backpack on the floor with a soft thud. "I wasn't sure where to go!" He glanced around at the other students, clearly another last-minute addition trying to get his bearings. "They switched me out of statistics yesterday—my advisor thought accounting was my future, but I couldn't handle all those numbers. Had to find something else fast."

Callum opened his mouth to respond and found he couldn't speak. Up close, the other student was even more striking—high cheekbones, full lips, and eyes that seemed to hold flecks of mischief even in the dim classroom lighting. There was something magnetic about him, something that made Callum want to stare and look away at the same time.

"You okay?" the young man asked, noticing Callum's frozen expression.

"Yes," Callum managed, his voice coming out rougher than intended. "I... yes. More than okay."

The smile that spread across his seatmate's face was warm and genuine, and Callum felt something shift in his chest—a recognition he wasn't ready to name, a door he'd never allowed himself to open.

"I'm Evan," the young man said, extending his hand. "Evan Thomas. The man with two first names."

"Callum," he replied, taking Evan's hand and feeling an electric jolt at the contact. "Callum Campbell."

"Nice to meet you, Callum Campbell," Evan said, and somehow made his ordinary name sound like something special.

Professor Henderson was explaining their first assignment—partnered scene work from contemporary plays—when Evan leaned closer and whispered, "You're cute. Want to work with me?" His breath was warm against Callum's ear, and there was something boldly direct in his tone that made Callum's pulse spike.

Callum had never had anyone speak to him like that—so forward, so confident, so... interested. Heat flooded his face, and he knew he was turning red. He opened his mouth to respond but no sound came out.

Evan's smile widened as he watched the blush spread across Callum's cheeks. "I'll take that as a yes," he whispered, clearly delighted by Callum's reaction.

Their quiet exchange hadn't gone unnoticed. Professor Henderson stopped mid-sentence, her attention drawn to the two students in the front row who were obviously not paying attention to her lecture on emotional authenticity.

"Gentlemen," she said, fixing them with a look that was part amusement, part annoyance. "Since you're clearly more interested in each other than in my explanation of scene work, perhaps you'd like to introduce yourselves to the class? We do have some new faces this week."

Callum felt his stomach drop. Every eye in the classroom turned toward them, and the heat in his face intensified from embarrassment to mortification. He reluctantly got to his feet, his legs feeling unsteady.

"I'm, uh, Callum Campbell," he managed, his voice barely above a mumble. "I'm a sophomore. From Owensboro." He sat down as quickly as possible, avoiding eye contact with anyone. A girl across the room gave him a small wave, and a few students nodded politely, but mostly they just looked mildly interested before turning their attention to Evan.

Evan stood with none of Callum's reluctance, flashing that infectious grin around the room as if he'd been waiting his whole life for this moment.

"I'm Evan Thomas," he announced with theatrical flair, "and I'm delighted to meet you all. Especially my new best friend here." He gestured toward Callum with a flourish that made several students chuckle and caused Callum to sink lower in his seat—though he couldn't quite suppress the secret thrill that ran through him at being claimed so publicly.

Professor Henderson raised an eyebrow but seemed amused rather than annoyed. "Well then, Mr. Thomas, Mr. Campbell, now that we've established your... friendship... perhaps we can get back to finding your authentic voices."

Evan settled back into his seat and leaned toward Callum

33

again. "I already found mine," he whispered, and Callum felt that same electric jolt from earlier, stronger this time, as if something inside him was waking up for the very first time.

Everything changed. Not dramatically, not with the crash of cymbals or the swell of orchestral music, but quietly—like the moment when winter finally gives way to spring and you realize the world has been transforming around you all along.

"This is going to be fun," Evan said, and Callum believed him completely.

Six

*When broken hearts
meet in the night,
and pain calls out to pain,
two souls might find
within their plight
the strength to heal
again.*

JAMES HAD SOMEHOW MANAGED to shuffle Callum back to the booth, uncertain of his steps and unsure what the outcome of this already terrible night would hold. It couldn't get much worse, he figured.

"Just... just stay there," James said, holding his hands out as if Callum might collapse at any moment. "I'll be right back. I'm just going to get you some water, okay?" He backed away slowly, as if Callum were made of glass, hoping his fragile composure would hold together long enough to help.

James turned and hurried behind the soda machine, grabbing a paper cup and pushing the water button. Nothing. "Dammit!" He'd already cleaned the machine and switched it to the locked position for the night.

"Hang on!" he called over to Callum, wanting to make sure he was still holding together. James ran to the office and grabbed the key, thinking absently that a soda machine with a lock seemed ridiculous as he fumbled with it.

"Here," James said, returning with the water. "Try to drink some of this." He held the cup out, and Callum grasped it with shaking hands, taking a small sip. He was still visibly upset but clearly coming back to the present moment.

James took the seat across from him, watching with worry etched across his young face.

Callum had looked as if he were somewhere else entirely, lost in another world. James recognized that look—he'd been having more of those moments lately, especially when he allowed himself to think about what had happened, trying to make sense of how everything had changed so slowly at first, then gained momentum until it all snowballed out of control.

He shook his head and gazed out the window at the snow, now clinging to the side of the building in thick, wet patches. Ironic, he thought.

Callum followed his gaze through the plate glass to the snow accumulating on the other side, then back to James. He looked down at the paper cup, now half-empty, and sat quietly. He was well beyond embarrassment about his breakdown. James seemed to have either forgotten about it entirely or was lost in his own thoughts, sitting in whatever mental space he'd retreated to.

Callum let out a weak attempt at a laugh and looked back at the young man sitting across from him, still gazing out the window. He watched James's eyes slowly begin to droop—not from exhaustion, though Callum suspected that was part of it.

No, it was as if his mind was allowing itself to drift back to whatever dark place it had been before Callum's outburst had interrupted.

"I'm so sorry, James," Callum finally whispered, his words pulling James back from wherever he'd been.

James shook his head quickly. "No, you're fine. I mean... it's Christmas, right? It's hard. I know."

It was James's halfhearted attempt to redirect them away from whatever precipice they'd both been standing on. He'd used variations of this response for weeks now, especially when people seemed surprised he couldn't make their Christmas parties or that he wasn't going home this year because his family was "too far away" and there was "school and all." He would assure them he'd be okay, that he understood their concern. "Christmas is tough on everyone sometimes," he would say, as if acknowledging their worry would make everything better.

Callum saw right through it.

"Why are you here?" Callum blurted out, his exhaustion bypassing the filter in his brain and going straight to the part that asked all the direct questions he normally kept to himself.

James looked as if Callum had slapped him. "I... I work here... and, uh..."

"No, I mean..." Callum's brain finally caught up with his mouth and tried to convince him to stop. "I'm sorry. I'm being nosy." He took the last sip of his water and shifted uncomfortably in his seat.

"It's... no, it's okay. I mean... do you want more water?" James saw an opportunity to deflect and change the subject. He'd gotten good at that lately. It was easier than answering questions no one really wanted honest answers to anyway.

"No, thank you." Callum looked down at the empty cup. "I mean..." He took a breath, his exhaustion once again bypassing his usual politeness. "Do you mind if I ask you something? You

can tell me it's none of my business and I'll leave. I should probably go anyway..."

"No." The word came out of James's mouth before he could
stop it, surprising them both. He paused, uncertain where that
had come from. "I mean... no, I don't mind. You can ask."

Why did you just say that? his brain immediately began
berating him. *It would be easier to get him out of here so you can
figure out where to sleep before...*

"Do you have anywhere to go when you finish your shift?"
Callum asked, then immediately realized how that sounded. "I
mean... I'm sorry. I'm just... well, not myself tonight."

James sat back slightly. Was this guy hitting on him?

"I meant... listen, I'm not trying to pick you up or anything,
if that's what you're thinking," Callum said quickly, trying to
correct himself. "I just... well, my gut tells me you're not prepared
for this storm, and sleeping in a car or on the street isn't..." He
trailed off, realizing he was way over the line. "Listen, I'm sorry.
This is none of my business, and I've already made a fool of
myself." He began sliding out of the booth for the second time
that evening.

"Please don't leave."

The words escaped James before he could stop them. *Where
did that come from?* he asked himself. *What the hell is going on in
your brain? Just shut up.* But something inside refused to listen.

"I... uh... well..." James couldn't get his words to make sense.
The struggle inside began taking a toll on the careful story he'd
constructed, the stoicism he'd told himself he needed to maintain. He moved his mouth, but nothing came out, and his eyes
began to well up.

No. No. No. No. He gripped his hands tightly, fighting not to
repeat Callum's earlier performance. *Just go. Just go so I can cry
alone. I don't need you to see this.*

Callum slid back into the booth, realizing he'd pushed too

38

hard. He'd known something was wrong from the moment he'd walked in, but maybe he shouldn't have said anything. It hurt to know his words were causing pain.

"I... I... uh..." James tried to speak, clawing back control. "I'm going to be... okay. Okay?" He fought to get through the sentence, never meeting Callum's eyes. If he had, he would have realized how much of a lie that was.

Callum sat quietly, allowing James to gather himself. He barely moved, just remained present.

Here we are, he thought.

There they were. Two strangers in a fast-food restaurant in the middle of a blizzard, both trying desperately not to fall apart, both failing, and somehow both still trying to take care of each other despite having nothing left to give.

Seven

Some truths come wrapped
in whispered word,
spoken to strangers
in the night,
because those who should have heard
have already turned
from sight.

"YOU KNOW," Callum began, deciding to ignore his rational self, "I met... someone... many years ago and..." He choked slightly, then practically willed heaven and earth to help him hold it together. "They... they..."

He had a choice to make—really, for himself. Did he take the easy route and use more euphemisms, more careful language to protect himself? Or did he just get it over with, pull the goddamn band-aid off already?

"They died." He paused, fighting for control. "They died last winter. It's... it's hard." He avoided James's gaze at all costs, looking frantically for anything to anchor him, his eyes landing on the pathetic Christmas tree doing its best to usher in tidings of comfort and joy.

James's eyes widened—not just because of the death, though he couldn't imagine losing someone important, but because of Callum's use of the word "they."

If it had been his wife, he surely would have said "her death," or better yet, used a name—"Susan's death" or "Jennifer's death." But he'd said "they," and James was still new to understanding the coded language of staying hidden, but he'd learned enough to recognize gay speak for "my partner" or "my boyfriend." Knowledge was power, he remembered Anders telling him at that Halloween party: "The less they know about you, the more power you have."

"I'm sorry," James said simply, unsure what else to offer.

Callum nodded slight appreciation, though he was tired of hearing those words. Why was everyone sorry? He wasn't sorry. He was angry. Evan had been stolen from him, pure and simple.

"I can't imagine what... what it must be like... especially now," James mumbled, but Callum heard every word. He'd been planning to draw out whatever was obviously troubling James by using his own pain to break the ice, but now James had turned the tables with one simple, heartfelt sentiment.

"No, you can't," Callum retorted automatically, then quickly caught himself at how bitter that sounded. "I didn't mean... well..."

"I've never had anyone... die."

God, how Callum hated that word. It was so final. So sharp.

He inhaled deeply and began again. "It's... a tremendous loss for me, especially when I have so many memories of him." Callum forgot himself in his honesty, and James caught the pronoun.

"Everyone just wants to be nice, trying to tell me to move on, to... oh, I don't know..." Callum's voice gained energy, frustration mixing with hurt. "I know they mean well, but they don't understand. I can't just forget him! I can't!" He teared up again, covering his eyes with his right hand, trying to dial it back.

James sat still, his own pain temporarily pushed aside as he watched this man's grief. Something in his chest began to unknot, his empathy reaching across the table.

"He sounds... you must have really loved him," James said softly.

Callum nodded, still holding his head in his hand before releasing it to show James a vulnerability he'd rarely let anyone see. His lip curled against a tear-streaked cheek, red and swollen, his nose running like he'd been out in the cold, his face grimacing as he fought to pull himself together, to be who he wanted people to see.

"I guess that's why I'm here. It's... I..."

"It's okay, Callum. You don't have to tell me anythi—"

"Yes! Yes, I do," Callum interrupted. "I need to tell someone. That's the problem—I haven't told anyone. Ever since... since..." He worked himself up again before the air deflated from his lungs. "Since Evan died."

They sat for what felt like the longest time—Callum focused on the twinkling lights on the tree by the door, James staring at Callum's hands, watching them twitch before he'd rub them, as if trying to calm himself.

"I'm sorry," Callum finally offered after gathering himself. He was still a wreck inside, but a tiny crack in his fortress had allowed just enough of this pain out that he felt the slightest relief. "I shouldn't have burdened you with this. It's..." He looked outside at the blowing snow, then up at the clock above the drive-through window. "11:23. It's late."

"It's okay. I have plenty of time. I'm... I'm happy to listen,"

43

James replied softly, and he meant it. He had nowhere to go anyway.

"Well, that's kind of you, and I feel embarrassed laying all this on you," Callum said, taking a pristine handkerchief from his inner coat pocket and wiping his eyes, cleaning his face back to respectability.

"Oh, no problem. I mean, Evan must have been really special for you to..."

Callum looked surprised. "Evan?"

James looked at him carefully. Had he said the wrong name?

"How... how did you know about Evan?"

"I... uh... I don't know him. You said his name."

"I did?" Callum suddenly realized his inhibitions must have completely fallen away during his breakdown.

"Yeah, but... it's okay. I won't tell," James said, trying to comfort him against any fear of being exposed. His default was to keep such things secret—bad things happened when secrets got out.

Callum looked a mixture of horrified and ashamed. His relationship with Evan had been carefully controlled—only a select few in their world knew about their love. And this kid had just heard him out everything about himself, about Evan, about his entire life in one carelessly spoken name. How could Evan's name be such a time bomb? He hated being this controlled, this careful, this...

James saw new emotions cross Callum's face—his entire body clenching, his shaking hands rolling into fists, not to strike but to defend. James recognized that look, that fear. He was living it daily.

"It's okay, Callum. I won't say anything. I know what it's like," James said, scrambling for the right words.

"How could you? Evan was—"

"No, I mean... I'm..." James became frantic, trying to land

this conversation safely but terrified he'd crash and burn. "I'm gay."

Callum stared at him, his fists suddenly releasing as the anxiety crossed the table and settled into James's body. James sat in near panic, visibly shaking.

"Oh, James... I didn't mean to force you to..." Callum started.

James's mouth was open, his eyes squinting as he looked away, searching for something to transport him somewhere else —somewhere he wasn't naked to the world, vulnerable, able to be hurt more than he already was.

Callum instinctively glanced around, looking for unwelcome ears nearby, just as he'd done for decades when it came to admitting these things. Of course they'd been alone since he'd arrived, but you could never be too careful. Not in the era of "Don't Ask, Don't Tell"—though unfortunately, most people did ask and wanted you to tell.

"James, I didn't mean to force you to—"

"It's okay. I just... get it," James said, fighting off sobs.

Callum reached across to take his hand, but James nearly bolted upright, frightened of any touch, his soul too wounded for contact.

"I'm sorry."

"No, don't be," Callum said, pulling his hand back and mentally chastising himself for the impulse.

"James," Callum said softly, forgetting his own worries to focus on this young man in their emotional ping-pong match.

"Mmm," James mumbled, his eyes firmly fixed on the Christmas tree.

"Has someone hurt you?"

James flinched as his mind replayed everything: his parents' slow disappearance from his life, his boyfriend being forced back to Pennsylvania, the couch-surfing, falling down in the world simply because he'd begun to fall in love.

All James could do was bite his lip and shake his head—not because he wasn't hurt, but because he wasn't sure where to begin. Or if he even wanted to.

"I wish I could help you," Callum whispered, sensing James was too fragile for much more.

"How?" James whispered back, almost like a dare. What could anyone do to fix the life he was now forced to live?

Callum wasn't sure, but he asked anyway: "Are you safe at home?" He noticed James flinch again at the word.

"I don't have one," James whispered, barely audible.

But Callum heard—as clearly as if James had shouted it. And he was pretty sure James didn't just mean a house, but everything home was supposed to mean: family, love, protection, joy, everything this season was supposed to embody. James had none of it.

Jesus, Callum thought. Evan had died—and God, maybe one day he'd be able to say that without breaking down—but at least Callum had a home. Empty, lonely, filled with painful memories, but still a home. He had friends who loved him, even if they pushed too hard sometimes. He had his position at the university, a beautiful house, years of accumulated wisdom. But James... this poor kid...

"James," Callum spoke gently. "Where are you staying?"

James kept his gaze on the tree, the twinkling lights giving him something to focus on instead of the reality that this stranger was getting too deep into his business. He couldn't let his guard down. Callum seemed nice, and he'd obviously been through terrible things, but James still didn't know him. What if he wanted something from James? He might have nothing left, but he wasn't going to... James's eyes began fighting against his will. God, he wished he could stop crying.

"Listen, James, I'm not trying to... do anything," Callum said, not knowing how to phrase it properly. How was he supposed to convince someone he truly cared? It seemed wrong

46

to have to clarify that kindness didn't come with strings attached.

James began to turn his head, looking Callum's way, skepticism mixing with pain.

"James, I don't expect you to believe me, and I know I haven't been in your situation, but..." Callum looked at the window, where snow was now clinging to form a white sheet. There was no way he was going to let this kid try to survive out there.

James followed his gaze and saw with dismay that the weather had gotten even worse.

"Listen, James... I have a home over on St. James Court. It's not far. It has guest rooms. You could have one just to stay warm. I promise the door locks, and I live on the second floor. I won't bother you..."

Callum was practically tongue-tied trying to put James's mind at ease, but it only came out in fragments. James wondered why he seemed so frantic. He'd never had a stranger offer to let him stay in their home—his upbringing had taught him that was tantamount to something perverted and wicked. But he saw something different in Callum's expression. He didn't seem like a predator. Still, didn't TV shows always feature the "nice man" who turned out to be a serial killer? And St. James Court—that was the wealthy area with all those big Victorian houses around the fountain, wasn't it?

"Thanks, but I..." James began, trying to end Callum's pleas.

"It's no trouble, James, really—"

"I appreciate it, really I do, but I already have a place to stay tonight," he lied. James had decided it was better to get Callum to leave. Sometimes it was easier to stick with what he knew, even if it hurt. Callum seemed nice, even generous, but the whole evening had been frightening, and he'd already said too much.

"You do?" Callum sounded dubious.

"Yeah, I've been staying with my friend." Which was true—he

had been, just not for the past few days, after realizing it would be better to leave. Sometimes words didn't need to be said for understanding to be perfectly clear.

"You are? It's pretty bad out there, James. Can I at least give you a ride?"

"No, thanks. He's going to come get me when I call, once I'm finished with my shift," James lied again.

Callum looked around and didn't see much else that James would need to do, but he exhaled in resignation.

"Okay, but..." Callum looked around, searching for something. "Do you have a paper and pen?"

James looked at him questioningly for a moment before nodding and retrieving them from behind the counter. Callum wrote down his address and phone number on the back of a torn receipt, sliding it across to James.

"This is where I live. You're always welcome to come by, anytime."

James took the paper and pushed it into his front pocket, nodding.

Callum recognized that nod—it was the same one his students gave when he offered advice or comments on their coursework. It really meant "I don't want to be rude, but whatever."

"I'm serious, James. You're welcome there any time, day or night. Please don't think you'd be an imposition."

James looked at him, wishing he would leave. He hated being rude to someone who was clearly trying to be kind, but it was hard to maintain his composure when Callum was being genuinely generous.

Callum stood, feeling like he should do something more. Hug James? No, that would be too much—the kid was scared of his own shadow. Shake his hand? What was he, someone's grandfather? He was only thirty-six, for Christ's sake. In the end, he just put on his gloves and pulled his coat tight as James let him back out into the winter.

"Remember, James. You have a place if you need it," he called back before disappearing into the blizzard where his car was hidden.

James had to pull the glass door tight against the wind trying to blow snow inside, then turned the lock, making sure no other lost strangers could stumble in. Going to the back, he flipped off the outside lights and walked to the time clock. He needed to punch out—otherwise he'd be in trouble for unauthorized overtime.

But once he did, the next clock would start ticking. Did he chance getting caught sleeping in the back again, or try to find shelter somewhere out there? He looked toward the window, where the storm showed no signs of stopping.

The piece of paper in his pocket felt heavier than it should have.

Eight

Before the fall comes pride,
before the winter,
spring—
some boys
must learn too late
what honesty can bring.

JAMES MCCARTHY HAD ALWAYS BEEN the center of attention, and he liked it that way. At St. Xavier High School, he'd been student body vice president, lacrosse captain, the kind of guy who could walk into any room and immediately know how to work it. His parents were prominent in Louisville's Catholic circles, and James had inherited their social confidence along with his father's strong jawline and his mother's expressive eyes.

College, however, was proving to be a different animal

entirely. At U of L, he was just another freshman in a sea of faces, his St. X reputation meaning nothing to kids from public schools across Kentucky who'd never heard of the McCarthy name. For the first time in his life, James was having to actually work to make friends.

Which was why, on a gray January morning in Professor Williams's American Literature class, James made it his business to be friendly to whoever ended up sitting near him. The lecture hall was filling up fast—it was a required course, and everyone needed to get it out of the way.

A guy slipped into the seat next to him just as Professor Williams began shuffling through his papers. James glanced over and saw someone about his own age, maybe slightly older, with light brown hair that looked like he'd tried to style it but gave up halfway through. He was wearing a rumpled button-down and jeans that had seen better days, and he had the kind of quietly attractive features that might go unnoticed in a crowd but were worth a second look up close.

The guy seemed nervous, clutching a notebook like it was a life preserver and avoiding eye contact with everyone around him. James recognized the type—probably from a small town, maybe first in his family to go to college, intimidated by the whole university experience.

"First time taking Williams?" James asked quietly as the professor launched into his syllabus explanation.

The guy looked startled, as if he hadn't expected anyone to talk to him. "Um, yeah. You?"

"Same. I'm James, by the way." He flashed his most disarming smile, the one that had gotten him elected to student council three years running.

"Ryan," the guy said, still looking uncertain. "Ryan Hoffman."

"Nice to meet you, Ryan Hoffman."

James had intended it to be a simple gesture of friendliness—
the kind of casual acquaintance-making that college required.
But over the following weeks, something about Ryan kept
drawing his attention. Maybe it was the way Ryan's face lit up
when he talked about a book he'd loved, or how he'd get so
absorbed in taking notes that he'd unconsciously bite his lower
lip, or the rare moments when he'd forget to be shy and let his
sharp sense of humor show.

James found himself looking forward to American Literature
in ways he'd never anticipated. He started arriving early to save
Ryan a seat, sharing his notes when Ryan's pen died, suggesting
they grab lunch after class. Ryan seemed perpetually surprised by
the attention, but also grateful for it.

"You don't have to sit with me, you know," Ryan said one
afternoon as they walked across campus together. "I'm sure you
have other friends to hang out with."

James considered this. He did have other friends—guys from
his dorm, people he'd met at orientation events. But none of
them made him feel the way Ryan did, though he couldn't have
articulated what that way was if pressed.

"I like hanging out with you," he said simply. "You're
different."

And he was. Ryan thought deeply about things in ways that
made James reconsider his own assumptions. He could analyze a
poem until it revealed layers James had never noticed, had opin-
ions about everything from music to politics that he was usually
too nervous to share until James drew them out of him.

"Want to be study partners for the midterm?" James asked
one day in early March. "We could go over our notes together,
maybe grab dinner in the dining hall."

Ryan looked like James had just offered him something
precious. "Really? You'd want to do that?"

"Of course. Why wouldn't I?"

That first study session led to regular meetings. James discovered that Ryan was brilliant in ways that weren't immediately obvious—he saw connections between ideas that James missed, remembered details that seemed insignificant until Ryan explained their importance. But more than that, Ryan listened when James talked, really listened, instead of just waiting for his turn to speak.

James started noticing other things too. The way Ryan's eyes would crinkle when he found something genuinely funny. How he'd unconsciously lean closer when he was trying to make a point. The careful way he'd choose his words, as if he were constantly editing himself.

"So do you have a girlfriend back home?" James asked one evening in April as they shared a pizza in Ryan's dorm room. It was the kind of casual question guys asked each other all the time, except Ryan's entire body went rigid.

"Not really," Ryan said carefully, not meeting James's eyes. "I mean, I dated someone for a while, but it didn't work out. What about you?"

"Similar story," James said, which was true enough. He'd taken girls to dances at St. X, had even kissed a few of them, but those experiences felt distant and abstract, like something he'd watched happen to someone else.

"Do you think you'll start dating again soon?" James asked, genuinely curious about Ryan's romantic life in a way that should have been a clue.

"I don't know," Ryan said, his voice tight. "Dating's... complicated."

James wanted to ask what he meant by that, but something in Ryan's tone suggested the conversation was over.

Similar exchanges happened throughout the spring—casual mentions of relationships that Ryan would deflect with vague pronouns and quick topic changes, leaving James increasingly puzzled. He found himself paying attention to the kinds of people Ryan looked at when they walked across campus, trying to figure out his type, but Ryan seemed to keep his gaze carefully neutral around everyone.

Meanwhile, James was becoming aware of something he couldn't quite name. His interest in dating had essentially evaporated since he'd started spending time with Ryan. When other guys pointed out attractive girls, James would nod and agree because that's what was expected, but his attention kept drifting back to the boy sitting next to him in literature class.

He caught himself studying Ryan's profile during lectures, memorizing the curve of his jaw and the way his eyelashes cast shadows on his cheeks. When Ryan smiled—really smiled, not the careful, polite version he showed most people—James felt something warm unfurl in his chest.

The realization, when it finally crystallized, hit James like cold water. He was attracted to Ryan. Not just as a friend, but as something more. The thought should have sent him into a panic —would have, if he'd let himself think about what it meant in terms of everything he'd been taught about himself, about what his parents expected, about what was acceptable in their world.

Instead, it mostly felt like finally understanding something that had been obvious all along.

By the end of spring semester, James had to face facts: he was falling in love with his best friend. And he had absolutely no idea what to do about it.

He spent the summer back in Louisville, working at his father's practice and trying to sort through his feelings. Ryan had returned to his family outside Covington, and they kept in touch with occasional phone calls—usually chit-chat about what each was doing, looking forward to being sophomores, typical college stuff.

Until one late night call in July when they got into a heated debate about which was the better amusement park: King's Island up in Cincinnati or Kentucky Kingdom right there in Louisville.

James, being a Louisville native, held firm to Kentucky Kingdom, even though he admitted The Beast at King's Island was incomparable. Ryan refused to budge from his beloved King's Island. He'd been there twice already that summer.

"You know what?" James said, suddenly inspired. "I should come up and go to King's Island with you one day, stay over, and then you come down and we'll hit Kentucky Kingdom. Settle this once and for all."

"Really?" Ryan sounded genuinely excited, and James felt that familiar warmth in his chest. "You'd want to do that?"

"Why not? It'll be fun."

James and Ryan were like two kids at King's Island, forgetting themselves as they hit every coaster. Late into the night, riding The Beast just before the park closed, they screamed and laughed, and James grabbed Ryan's hand to force him to raise his arms while going down the second hill. The contact was electric, and James found he didn't want to let go. They held hands all the way back to the gate, neither speaking about it during the euphoria of the moment.

It wasn't until they were walking toward the parking lot that Ryan seemed to realize their fingers were still intertwined. He pulled away suddenly, a blush spreading across his cheeks in the parking lot lights.

James felt the loss of contact like a physical ache, but he just smiled. "That was incredible."

"Yeah," Ryan said quietly, not quite meeting his eyes. "It was."

The next day they drove down to Louisville for Kentucky Kingdom. It was smaller than King's Island, sure, but James had so many childhood memories there. He found himself grabbing

Ryan's hand often to drag him to various rides, telling him stories about what each one meant to him, the history of the place. Ryan seemed to notice how comfortable James was with touching him—nothing inappropriate, but a casual intimacy that went beyond typical male friendship.

They spent time in the water park too, floating around the lazy river in the afternoon heat. James caught Ryan looking at him when he thought James wasn't paying attention—quick glances that made James's pulse quicken and confirmed what he'd been wondering about all summer.

Ryan spent a couple of days with the McCarthy family, and James's parents were charmed by him. His polite manners and obvious intelligence impressed James's father, while his thoughtfulness and genuine interest in her garden won over James's mother. Watching Ryan fit so seamlessly into his family life made something settle in James's chest that he hadn't even realized was unsettled.

When it came time for Ryan to return to Covington, James felt genuinely bereft.

"I had a really good time," Ryan said as they stood by his car, both of them seemingly reluctant for the visit to end.

"Me too," James said. "Really good."

There was a moment when they just looked at each other, and James thought Ryan might say something more. But then Ryan just nodded and got in his car, leaving James standing in his driveway with a thousand unspoken words on his tongue.

The idea came to James a few days later, as he was dreading the thought of returning to dorm life with its lack of privacy and constant noise.

"What would you think about getting an apartment together this year?" he asked during their next phone call.

There was silence on the other end of the line.

"As roommates, I mean," James added quickly. "It would be cheaper than the dorms, and we already know we get along."

"I..." Ryan sounded uncertain. "Do you really think that's a good idea?"

"Why wouldn't it be?"

Another pause. "I don't know. It's just... different. Living together."

James could hear the worry in Ryan's voice, and he suspected it had to do with the same undercurrents that had been building between them all summer. The hand-holding, the glances, the way they seemed to orbit each other with increasing gravity.

"We're already friends," James said gently. "This would just be... practical."

"What about your parents? And mine?"

That was the bigger hurdle. The apartment discussion happened right after Ryan's visit, but both sets of parents had immediate concerns. James's parents worried about him living off-campus as just a sophomore—too much independence too soon. Ryan's parents had similar reservations, though James suspected their concerns were more financial than philosophical.

It took the rest of July and into August to convince them. James made careful arguments about responsibility and cost savings, while Ryan handled the practical research—finding available apartments, calculating expenses, proving they could manage the responsibility. James suspected his parents were swayed partly by the fact that they liked and trusted Ryan, seeing him as a stabilizing influence rather than a corrupting one.

If they only knew, James thought, and then pushed the thought away before he could examine what exactly they might know.

By mid-August, they'd found a small two-bedroom place near campus and gotten both sets of parents to co-sign the lease. James told himself it was just a practical arrangement between friends, a way to save money and gain independence before their sophomore year began.

But as he packed his belongings in late August and prepared to move in with Ryan, James couldn't shake the feeling that he was about to cross a line he'd never be able to uncross.

He just wasn't sure if that terrified or thrilled him more.

Nine

~~

Between the memory
of warmth
and winter's
killing bite,
a boy walks toward the past
to freeze
alone tonight.

JAMES PULLED his winter coat tighter as he stepped out into the storm, immediately regretting his decision. The wind cut through the fabric like it wasn't there, and within minutes his exposed hands were already numb. The tennis shoes he'd managed to keep when he'd been forced out of his apartment were no match for the accumulating snow and ice—within a block, they were soaked through, his feet squishing with each step through the frozen slush.

The backpack containing what few clothes he'd been able to

salvage bounced against his spine, throwing off his balance as he tried to navigate the dark streets. He'd thought he could make it to campus, maybe slip into one of the dorms when someone unlocked a door, crash on a common room sofa until morning. It had seemed manageable from inside the warm restaurant.

But the storm was much worse than he'd expected. As he trudged through the accumulating snow, he was surprised to see Interstate 65 completely shut down, red and blue lights flickering through the blowing flakes from police cars positioned to block the on-ramps. If they were closing the highways, this was serious.

By the time he reached the dorms, it was well after midnight, and there was little protection from the relentless weather. He walked from building to building, hoping to find someone coming in late, but most students had either already left for the holiday break or were safely tucked inside, too smart to venture out in this weather. The longer he waited—jumping from foot to foot outside the entrances, hoping someone would see him and take pity—the more he realized this plan was hopeless.

He could barely feel his feet anymore, and stuffing his hands deep into his coat pockets only seemed to make them sting slightly less. The wind was the worst part, cutting right through his jeans, which seemed to be both wet and frozen at the same time.

Then he remembered the Halloween party. That house on Brooke Street where he and Ryan had walked that night two months ago. The roommates had seemed so kind, so welcoming. Maybe they'd still be awake, maybe they'd remember him. It wasn't that far—he and Ryan had walked it easily enough that October night.

James turned west, pushing through the blown snowdrifts toward Old Louisville. The Victorian houses loomed dark and imposing in the storm, and by the time he reached Brooke Street, he could barely see through the whiteout conditions. The street was completely abandoned, porch lights either turned off or lost in the swirling snow.

He couldn't remember which house it was. They all looked the same in the darkness, and his body had begun shivering—not the performative kind you do to show others how cold you are, but the deep, involuntary response you can't control. The kind you don't even realize is happening until you can no longer walk properly.

James looked around desperately, knowing he needed to find shelter from the wind more than anything. Turning down an alleyway illuminated by a single streetlamp fighting to pierce through the blizzard, he found a slight alcove tucked into one of the old carriage house garages. A small overhang covered what had once been a door, flanked by hedgerows taller than him that offered some protection from the wind.

He was exhausted from walking miles—from the restaurant, through campus, and now through Old Louisville. His legs ached, his arms wouldn't stop quivering. He told himself he just needed to rest for a moment, just needed to get out of the wind and regroup, figure out what to do next.

If he nestled down against the hedge, pulled his legs up to his chest and leaned back against the covered doorway, he could rest for a bit. He was so tired—he'd been awake for almost nineteen hours. Maybe he could just sleep for a moment.

Just for a moment.

"Come on, James, it'll be fun!" Ryan was practically bouncing with excitement as they walked down Brooke Street, looking for the address his friend had given them.

James adjusted his Batman cowl nervously. "You're sure this is going to be okay? I mean, this is a... gay party, right? It's not going to be like... sex and drugs and stuff?"

Ryan laughed, the sound muffled by his Robin mask. "Where do you get this stuff? It's just a party."

But James only knew the stereotypes—what his church had said about homosexuals, the "love the sinner, hate the sin" rhetoric that had been a constant theme since he and Ryan had first kissed a month ago. Every time they were physical, it felt both completely right and somehow wrong, leaving him with a guilt he couldn't shake.

"My friend's boyfriend got the invite from one of the room-mates," Ryan assured him. "Costumes required. 'Come dressed to impress,' they said. 'No half-ass store-bought shit.'" He gestured to their elaborate costumes, rented from the theater company downtown for forty-five dollars each. It had been a lot of money, but they'd wanted to make a good impression.

The house, when they found it, was nothing like James had expected. Instead of some seedy gathering, it looked like some-thing out of a magazine—lights stringing the wraparound porch, professionally carved jack-o'-lanterns, the sound of laughter and music drifting from the windows.

The door was answered by someone in an elaborate Endora costume—the mother witch from Bewitched—complete with towering hair and dramatic makeup. James and Ryan had never seen the show, but the effect was stunning.

"Welcome, darlings!" Endora swept them into the house with open arms, and James found himself being hugged by a complete stranger. It was odd, but kind of nice—he noticed everyone seemed to hug each other here.

Inside, James's preconceptions crumbled entirely. There were no kegs or beer pong tables like at the frat parties he'd avoided. Instead, there was an actual bartender serving cocktails in proper glasses, little pumpkins and skulls replacing the tiny umbrellas.

The entire house was decorated like a professional production—themed music, elaborate lighting, every detail carefully considered.

"This must have cost a fortune," James whispered to Ryan as they took in the scene.

People moved through the rooms in stunning costumes—some that could have walked off a Hollywood set. James and Ryan found Ryan's friend and his boyfriend dressed as a mummy and Egyptian pharaoh, the latter's exposed chest catching James's attention before he quickly looked away, embarrassed by the attraction he felt.

Everyone seemed so comfortable, so at ease. James whispered to Ryan, "I can't believe everyone here is actually... gay. Like, real gay people." It was nothing like he'd expected. They were open, holding hands, being themselves. When a couple kissed right in front of them, Ryan smiled at James knowingly.

They joined a group on the back porch bobbing for apples, laughing as the winner—soaked through his ghost costume—was awarded an actual trophy by someone in wizard robes and a pointy hat.

When Ryan went to get them drinks, James made his way upstairs to a quieter family room where a few people sat talking. The TV was showing Poltergeist, the static hissing "They're here!" as he settled on the edge of the sofa.

The wizard from the apple game appeared in the doorway. "Having a good time?" he asked, crossing to take the oversized armchair beside James.

James nodded, and the wizard extended his hand. "I'm Anders," he said. "And you're Batman, right?"

They both laughed at the obviousness of it.

Anders noticed James seemed a little overwhelmed sitting alone. "Are you here by yourself?"

"No, my... uh... friend is getting drinks downstairs."

Anders nodded knowingly. "Friend." He'd used that term many times himself. But this was a safe space. "You mean your boyfriend?" he asked, completely comfortable and without judgment.

James went red-faced. He'd never said he was gay aloud to anyone—not even Ryan, really. Well, he'd asked Ryan if they were boyfriends after that first kiss, so naive and sweet, but never to anyone else.

"It's okay, James. I'm gay—we all are around here. And those who aren't are cool with it. They get it."

James's shyness persisted, but Anders continued gently. "You a student?"

"Yeah, sophomore. You?"

"No, graduated last year. I live here with two other room-mates. Moved in last January."

"Really? Where'd you go to school?"

"Art school in Chicago."

James was intrigued—he'd never known any real artists. "What happened? I mean, why Louisville? Chicago's so cool and..."

He saw the slightest hint of sadness cross Anders's face before he responded with practiced positivity. "Well, I got kicked out by my dad."

James's eyes widened. "What? How?"

Anders was used to this question, but it still hurt. "He found out about my boyfriend, Patrick. You know... didn't want a fag for a son, all that." He tossed it off like yesterday's news, but James could see it still got to him.

"He kicked you out?"

"It's fine, really. My roommate said, 'Well, fuck him!' and told me to come live with them." Anders laughed, and James half-giggled, unsure if that was appropriate. "I uprooted my life, moved here in January, got a job."

"January?" James couldn't imagine being homeless at Christmas.

"Yeah, Dad caught us right after Christmas."

"What happened to Patrick?" The question slipped out before James could stop it.

Anders's tone shifted slightly. "Oh, well... he didn't want to move to Louisville. We're still friends, I hope."

James dropped the subject, sensing deeper pain there.

"It's okay," Anders continued, sweeping his arms to indicate the party around them. "I'm in a much better place anyway. Everyone here pretty much has the same story—we've all gotten shit from our families. Being gay isn't easy sometimes, you know?"

James felt his stomach twist. He'd been so focused on his own guilt about his attraction to Ryan that he hadn't really considered what admitting it publicly could cost him.

"But that's why we throw these parties," Anders said, brightening. "It's my fifth this year alone. You should've seen the Derby party!"

James still looked worried, and Anders noticed. "It's okay, James. We're like a little family here. We try to take care of each other—like my roommates helped me, I try to help others. No one else will."

Just then Ryan appeared with drinks and snacks. "There you are!"

"This is Anders," James said as Anders helped Ryan balance everything.

"James here has been telling me all about you!" Anders said, winking at James, who blushed.

"He has?" Ryan looked puzzled.

"Yep! Said he had the cutest boyfriend here and I can see why!"

Ryan smiled and looked at James affectionately while James turned even redder.

"Well, I need to make the rounds," Anders said. "It was nice meeting you both."

After he left, Ryan asked, "Who was that?"

James told him about Anders's story, and they both winced at the idea of being thrown away by family like garbage.

"He seems really nice though," Ryan said finally. "Like he's doing well."

"Yeah," James nodded, still imagining what Anders had gone through. He couldn't picture his own father doing that, but then again, he didn't plan on letting him find out about Ryan anytime soon. Ryan was still just his best friend, officially.

"Want to go downstairs? They're organizing a trick-or-treat group."

James laughed at the absurdity of adults going trick-or-treating, but found the idea amusing enough to want to see it. "Sure, let's go."

Ryan grabbed his hand naturally, and they made their way back to the crowd, James feeling a warmth that had nothing to do with the house's heating system.

Ten

When pride meets shame
in one cruel moment,
and love becomes
a weapon used,
the heart learns how quickly joy
can turn to
everything that's bruised.

CALLUM BARELY MADE IT HOME, sliding through unplowed snow drifts and inching along Fourth Street before finally turning onto St. James Court and down the narrow alley toward his garage. It was a miracle he could even get the door open in this weather. He made his way through the back entrance of his house—empty feeling, as always—and found himself wondering how James was managing.

He suspected James hadn't been entirely honest about having a place to stay, but he'd seemed so adamant about it. What could

Callum have done? Force a strange young man to come home with him? That would have been healthy, he thought sarcastically as he thrust his key into the frozen back door lock, jiggling it to break the ice free before entering the warm sanctuary of the converted summer kitchen he and Evan had turned into an atrium a few years back.

Wrestling off his snow-covered coat and kicking off his saturated shoes, he hurried into the kitchen and instinctively flipped on the electric kettle—a ritual Evan had begun, always wanting something hot in winter regardless of the time of day. But he didn't actually want anything. He didn't drink coffee, and it was far too late for tea. Flipping the switch back off, he turned out the lights and made his way toward the front of the house.

They had bought the place simply for the staircase. Everything else could have been replaced, but the grand stairwell was irreplaceable, and Evan would have overruled any objections Callum might have had about purchasing the house. Truth be told, Callum had loved it just as much, but he'd kept a stoic attitude with the realtor—no need to show all his cards.

Tonight, Callum stopped and crossed to look through the side window by the front door. The heavy, old door was the kind you'd find in London's Mayfair district—it really made the house. But now the transom was nothing more than a landing spot for blowing snow. He peered outside, hoping perhaps James might show up after all, but there were no footsteps in the snow, no young man seeking shelter.

It was no surprise, really. James wouldn't have been foolish enough to walk through this storm, Callum told himself as he turned toward the staircase. No one would walk through this weather.

Still, he couldn't shake his worry.

❄

"Let's crash the party at The Brown!" someone shouted as the group of trick-or-treaters made their way down the street, paper bags half-full of candy and spirits high from their successful neighborhood adventure.

James looked at Ryan uncertainly. They'd been having such a wonderful time with Anders and the others from the Brooke Street house—everyone so welcoming, so accepting. James had felt more comfortable being himself in the past few hours than he had in months. But crashing a fancy hotel party seemed like pushing their luck.

"Come on," Ryan said, squeezing James's hand. "We're in costume. Who's going to know?"

One of their new friends, dressed as a pharaoh, grinned. "My friend works the front desk sometimes. Says there's always some charity thing going on. Rich people love their costume parties."

The Brown Hotel's grand ballroom was everything James had imagined from movies—crystal chandeliers, elaborate decorations, people in expensive costumes mingling with champagne flutes. The fundraiser was clearly a high-society affair, but in their rented Batman and Robin costumes, they blended in surprisingly well.

"This is incredible," James whispered to Ryan as they made their way to one of the lavishly decorated refreshment tables. The entire scene felt like something from another world—his world, actually, the world of his parents' charity events, but experienced now through completely different eyes.

Ryan was animated, pointing out costumes, grabbing James's hand to drag him toward different displays. The atmosphere was infectious, and James found himself relaxing more than he had all evening. When Ryan pulled him close and gave him a quick kiss as they laughed at someone's elaborate peacock costume, it felt natural, spontaneous—just another moment of joy in what had become a magical night.

That's when everything changed.

"Excuse me." The voice was sharp, authoritative. "How did you young men gain entry to this event?"

James turned to see a man in elaborate bishop's robes approaching, flanked by several other well-dressed adults. At first, James thought it was just another costume—an impressively authentic one—but the man's tone suggested otherwise.

"This is a Catholic Charities fundraiser," the bishop continued, his voice carrying the kind of moral authority James recognized from years of Sunday sermons. "Not some... heathen gathering."

Others were gathering around them now—a small crowd drawn by the commotion. James's eyes swept over them, taking in the expensive costumes, the suspicious stares. That's when he saw him.

The man in the James Bond tuxedo standing directly across from them, his face a mask of dawning recognition. Their eyes met, and James felt his world tilt on its axis.

Dad.

His father's gaze traveled downward, landing on James's hand, which was still intertwined with Ryan's. The moment stretched between them like a held breath, and James saw everything he needed to see in his father's face: shock, understanding, and then something that looked very much like disgust.

James pulled his hand away from Ryan's as if it had burned him, but it was too late. His mother appeared beside his father, curiosity shifting to confusion as she tried to understand what was happening.

"James?" she said uncertainly, as if she couldn't quite believe what she was seeing.

But James was already moving, turning away from his parents, from the bishop, from the crowd of staring faces. He ran through the ballroom, past the elaborate decorations and disapproving looks, through the hotel lobby and out into the night.

He ran across Broadway without waiting for the light, barely missing a city bus, then through the streets with no conscious destination except *away*—away from that look in his father's eyes, away from the moment when his two worlds had collided with devastating consequences.

His feet carried him back toward the only place that had felt safe that night: the Brooke Street house where people had accepted him without question.

The phone rang once, then stopped. A moment later, it rang again.

Callum thought he was dreaming. Why wouldn't someone answer the damn phone? Evan?

He shot upright as it rang a third time and grabbed the receiver.

"Mr. Campbell?"

The voice sounded like something from a movie, only worse because it was real.

"This is Sergeant Rodriguez with the Louisville Police."

"Police? Is something wrong?"

"Mr. Campbell, do you have a son?"

"A son? No, I'm... single." Even in his sleep-addled state, Callum knew how to deflect questions about why he didn't have a wife or family.

"Well, we found a young man. He had your name and address on a slip of paper in his pocket."

James. "What happened? Where is he?"

"How do you know the young man? He didn't seem to have a wallet or any identification we could find."

Callum tried not to sound guilty. "I... he was working at Wendy's when I stopped by earlier. We talked."

"I see. Do you know his last name?"

"I... no, I only got his first name. From his name tag."

Callum could hear the officer writing. "Mr. Campbell, can you explain why he had your contact information in his pocket?"

Here it was. Callum couldn't lie—it wasn't in his nature—but he didn't want to sound like some predator either.

"He... well, he essentially confessed he was homeless, and I offered to help him."

"Mm-hmm."

"He turned me down—I didn't blame him. He didn't know me. But it was terrible weather, and..."

"So you gave him your address in case he changed his mind?"

"Yes. I know it seems strange, but... it being Christmas and all..." Callum cringed at using that phrase, the same one people had been using on him all season to try to cheer him up.

"Of course. Kind of you." The officer seemed to accept this. "Can you tell me anything else? Anything that would help us notify his parents or next of kin?"

Something in the phrasing made Callum's stomach drop. "Is he... is he okay?"

The officer paused. "We found him nearly frozen to death in an alley not far from your home. He's at University Hospital. I don't have information on his current status."

"Oh, Jesus," Callum whispered.

"We think he may have been trying to make his way to your house when he had to take shelter."

The guilt hit Callum like a physical blow. He should have insisted. Should have refused to take no for an answer.

"Is he going to be okay?"

"I don't have that information, Mr. Campbell. I'm trying to locate his family."

Callum suspected, based on their conversation, that James's family wouldn't be particularly receptive to being "located."

"I'm sorry. He didn't share much with me. I wish he had."

"If you think of anything—something he might have said—"

"Yes, of course. I'm going to head over to the hospital now."

"I'm not sure you'll be able to see him, given his condition—"

"He's still alive?" Callum's voice cracked.

"Last I heard, he was being transported there. That's all I know."

After hanging up, Callum sat on the edge of his bed, fully awake and in panic mode. University Hospital. Didn't he know someone there?

He flipped through his bedside Rolodex with shaking fingers.

"Rich, thank God you answered." Callum paced his bedroom, the cordless phone pressed to his ear. "I need you to check on someone who should be coming into the ER."

Ryan nearly caught up with James just as he reached the front steps of the Brooke Street house, where the party continued with fewer people but undiminished warmth. James was sobbing, inconsolable, unable to explain even to himself exactly what he was feeling, let alone thinking.

Anders noticed something through the downstairs window and appeared on the porch, curious. Some of the trick-or-treaters returning, perhaps?

He found James doubled over on the front stoop, Ryan sitting beside him with an arm around his shoulders, trying to get him to calm down. Anders stepped around them both and knelt on the sidewalk in front of James.

"What happened?" He knew better than to ask if anything was wrong—that was obvious.

James was beyond words, his breath coming in ragged gasps between sobs.

Ryan tried to explain through his own panic. "James's dad... caught us... we were at this party at The Brown..."

"What?"

Between Ryan's fragmented explanations and James's broken attempts to speak, Anders pieced together enough to understand this wasn't something to be taken lightly. He'd lived through his own version of this nightmare.

Without a word, he went inside and returned with a glass of water and a box of tissues.

"James," he said gently, practically forcing the glass into James's shaking hands. "Drink this."

Ryan seemed reluctant to let go, his protective instincts in overdrive, but Anders gently suggested he go splash some water on his own face. "James needs some breathing space. He'll be okay. I promise."

After Ryan reluctantly went inside, Anders took his place on the stoop beside James, who stared through his tears at the night, gripping the water glass like a lifeline.

Anders didn't speak—just nudged James's shoulder gently, letting him know he was there while giving him space to process.

Slowly, words began tumbling out: "Dad... caught... life ruined... over... can't..." Anders listened patiently, occasionally encouraging James to drink, to breathe.

When James had emptied the glass, Anders set it aside and let him continue. The story came in fragments—having fun, didn't see his dad, Catholic charity ball, Ryan kissed him, got caught, his father's eyes...

James broke down again, and Anders understood completely. The trauma, the fear, the shame—it brought back vivid memories of his own father's reaction, the violence, the rejection.

When James finally collapsed against his chest, holding on as if his life depended on it, Anders embraced him, gently rocking him, letting him release years of compressed fear and vulnerability into the night.

Ryan stood in the doorway behind them, watching. This night hadn't gone in any direction he'd expected.

Not at all.

Eleven

In the shadow of last goodbyes,
where grief sits heavy,
cold,
sometimes a chance to save someone
helps heal
what can't be told.

"RICH, THANK GOD YOU ANSWERED." Callum clutched the phone, his hand trembling slightly. "I need to ask about someone who should have come into the ER tonight."

Dr. Richard Brennan's voice was tired and confused. "Cal? Jesus, what time is it? It's not even..." he looked at his watch..." God, Cal... it's only three. Everything okay?"

"I'm fine. I need to know about a patient, a young man, probably brought in with hypothermia. Tonight."

"Hypothermia?" Rich's voice sharpened with professional

alertness. "Cal, why are you calling me about a patient? That's not exactly protocol, and frankly, it's been a hell of a night. We've had three major cases come through because of this storm, and..."

"Please, Rich. This is important."

"Important how? Do you know this person? Because I can't just give out patient information to..."

"His name is James." Callum's voice cracked. "Eighteen, nineteen... twenty at best. Dark hair. He might not have had ID with him."

Rich went quiet for a moment. When he spoke again, his voice was different, more focused, concerned. "Cal, how do you know about this kid?"

"So he is there?"

"Answer my question first. How do you know him?"

Callum closed his eyes. "I met him tonight. He works at Wendy's...worked there. He's homeless, Rich, and I tried to help, but he wouldn't let me."

"Okay, slow down. You met him tonight and..."

"I gave him my address. Told him he could come by if he needed help." The words tumbled out. "I should have made him come with me then. I should have insisted instead of just—"

"Wait, wait." Rich's voice became sharp with understanding. "Your address? Cal, we found a piece of paper in his pocket with an address on it. I didn't piece together that it was yours. The officers were trying to figure out if it was family or..."

"It was mine." Callum's voice was barely a whisper.

"Jesus Christ." Rich was quiet for a long moment. "Cal, this kid was nearly dead when they brought him in. Core temperature was down to 84 degrees. Another hour in that alley and..."

"Is he going to be okay?"

Rich paused, thinking of his word carefully. "We got him stabilized. He's warming up, but we're monitoring for complications." Rich's voice softened. "Cal, what the hell is going on? Since when do you hand out your address to homeless kids?"

How could Callum explain without sounding like he was collecting strays? "He reminded me of..." Callum stopped. Of Evan at that age. Lost and trying so hard to seem okay. "He was scared, Rich. Really scared. And I let him walk away into this storm."

"And he was trying to get to your house?"

"I think so. The officer said they found him in an alley not far from my neighborhood."

Rich sighed heavily. "This is the kid with no family, no emergency contacts. We've been trying to figure out what to do with him when he's discharged."

"I'm coming down there."

"Cal, the roads are—"

"I'm coming, Rich. He doesn't have anyone else."

"Listen to me. I can't just let you walk into the ICU to see some random kid. There are protocols, and even with the storm, there are supervisors around. I could get in serious trouble."

"Please Rich." The desperation in Callum's voice was raw. "He was trying to reach me when this happened. That.. that has to count for something."

There was a long silence. When Rich spoke again, his voice was different—softer, more personal. "Cal, you sound like... when was the last time I heard you this upset about someone?"

The answer hung between them. Not since Evan. Not since those final months when Callum had fought hospital bureaucracy, visiting hours, everything that stood between him and the person he loved.

"He's just a kid, Rich. Nineteen, maybe twenty. He was so scared tonight, and I.. I let him walk away."

Rich sighed heavily. "If you can make it through this

weather... I'll figure something out. But I'm sticking my neck out here, and if anyone asks questions..."

"I understand."

"And Cal? Drive carefully. I don't want to treat you for hypothermia too."

The journey took nearly an hour through streets that should have been abandoned. Callum's car slid constantly despite his careful driving, and twice he had to stop and clear ice from his wipers. By the time he reached University Hospital, his hands were numb and his nerves frayed.

The ER was eerily quiet compared to its usual chaos. A skeleton crew moved between rooms, and the storm had kept all but the most serious cases away. Callum approached the reception desk, where a woman looked up from her charts.

"I'm here about the hypothermia patient. I'm Callum Campbell."

She frowned. "Are you family?"

The question caught him off guard. "Dr. Brennan is expecting me."

"Let me page him."

Rich appeared a few minutes later, looking harried. His usually neat hair was disheveled, and there were coffee stains on his scrubs.

"Cal." He glanced around the waiting area, then gestured toward a quiet corner. "Look, this is complicated."

"How is he?"

Rich took a breath. "Better. Temperature is normal, circulation is good. We're monitoring for complications, but he should recover fully." Rich ran a hand through his hair. "I want to keep an eye out on his hands and feet, but that's not the problem."

"What do you mean?"

"No wallet, no ID—nothing. Police only found that crumpled piece of paper with your address." Rich rubbed his forehead.

"We can't verify his age, can't contact family. Legally, if he's under eighteen, we need a guardian to make medical decisions. If he's of age..." Rich lowered his voice. "This kid is a ghost, Cal. He'll probably be ready for discharge tomorrow—assuming his hands and feet look good, but we can't just put him back on the street."

"Can I see him?"

Rich was quiet for a long moment, clearly wrestling with hospital policy versus personal loyalty. "I could lose my job for this. Patient privacy, visiting restrictions—there are a dozen reasons I should say no."

"But?"

"But I haven't seen you care about anything since Evan died. And this kid..." Rich shook his head. "He doesn't have anybody. Just you, asking about him in the middle of a blizzard. I... well, I can't just let him... five minutes, okay?"

They looked at each other, years of friendship weighing the balance.

"Five minutes," Rich said again. "If anyone asks, you helped get him to the hospital. That's it."

The ICU was dimly lit, filled with the soft symphony of monitors and ventilators. Rich led Callum to a room at the end of the hall, where James lay small and still in the hospital bed.

He looked impossibly young, his dark hair stark against white pillows. Both hands were wrapped in gauze, and angry red patches of frostbite marked his cheekbones. Various machines tracked his vital signs with steady electronic beeps.

"He's sedated," Rich said quietly. "Won't wake up for several hours."

Callum pulled a chair up beside the bed, his legs suddenly weak. "God, he's just a baby."

"Cal." Rich's voice was careful. "What's the plan here? Because when he wakes up, he's going to need somewhere to go. And kids who've been surviving on their own..."

"Don't trust easily," Callum finished. "I know."

"So what happens next?"

Callum looked at James's peaceful face, at the bandaged hands that had been frozen trying to reach safety. "I don't know. I just know he was trying to get to my house when this happened."

Rich studied his friend's expression—the fierce protectiveness, the determination. It was the first real emotion he'd seen from Callum since the funeral.

"I need to check my other patients," Rich said finally. "You've got a few more minutes."

Alone with James, Callum felt the weight of responsibility settling on his shoulders. This boy had trusted him enough to seek help, had nearly died trying to reach the address on that crumpled piece of paper.

"I don't know if you can hear me," Callum said quietly, his voice catching. "But what happened tonight... God, kid, I'm so sorry."

James's breathing remained steady, unchanged, but Callum's hands clenched in his lap as he stared at the bandaged fingers he couldn't touch.

"I should have made you come with me. Should have..." He stopped, his throat tight. "I have this house, see? Too big for just me. Way too big. And I know..." His voice broke completely. "I know what it's like when nobody gives a damn about you."

He leaned forward in his chair, desperate to reach out but afraid of disturbing the IV lines, the monitors, all the fragile machinery keeping James stable.

"So if no one else cares about you, kid... if your family won't..." Callum's voice dropped to a fierce whisper as he wiped his eyes, "Then I will. I don't know how, but I will."

Outside, the storm continued, but here in this small room, James was safe and warm. Watching the steady rise and fall of the boy's chest, Callum felt something he hadn't experienced in months—the sense that he was needed for something important, larger than himself.

He settled back in his chair to wait, remembering the last time he'd sat beside a hospital bed—watching Evan's final breaths, powerless to save him. This time felt different.

This time, he could do something.

Twelve

When morning breaks
on borrowed time,
and strangers hold your fate,
sometimes
the hardest thing to do
is let someone else
care.

JAMES'S first conscious thought was that his hands were on fire.

The second was that he didn't recognize the ceiling above him—smooth white tiles with recessed lighting, nothing like the water-stained drop ceiling of the Wendy's back room where he'd been sleeping. Panic shot through him as he tried to sit up, only to discover his arms were tethered to machines by clear plastic tubes.

"Easy there." A woman in scrubs appeared beside his bed, her voice gentle but professional. "You're in the hospital. You're safe."

Hospital. The word hit him like a physical blow. Hospitals meant bills he couldn't pay, questions he couldn't answer, forms requiring information he didn't have. His mind raced as he tried to piece together how he'd gotten here.

"My backpack," he said, his voice coming out as a rasp. "Where's my backpack?"

The nurse—Maria, according to her name tag—checked his chart. "You didn't have any belongings when you were brought in. Just the clothes you were wearing."

James's stomach dropped. His wallet, his ID, what little money he'd saved—everything had been in that backpack. "I need to call someone. I need to—"

"First, let's make sure you're okay." Maria checked the machines around his bed with practiced efficiency. "Do you remember what happened?"

Fragments came back: leaving the restaurant, the walk through campus, the growing cold. Brooke Street. Looking for Anders's house—the only place he'd felt welcome since Halloween. Then nothing.

"I was... I got lost in the storm." It wasn't exactly a lie.

"You have some frostbite on your hands and feet, but you're lucky. Another hour out there..." She didn't finish the sentence. "The police found you in an alley around three this morning."

James stared at his bandaged hands, trying to process. Three in the morning. He'd been unconscious for hours.

"Now," Maria said, pulling up a chair, "we need to get some information from you. Starting with your full name and date of birth."

The questions he'd been dreading. James gave his name and birthdate—October 15, 1977. Nineteen years old, barely.

"Address?"

This was where it got complicated. "I... I'm between addresses right now."

Maria's pen paused. "Emergency contact?"

James was quiet for a long moment. His parents' number was burned into his memory, but calling them would be worse than dying in that alley. "I don't have one right now."

"Parents' contact information?"

"No." The word came out sharper than he intended.

Maria set down her pen and studied his face. She'd clearly seen this before—young patients with no family willing to claim them. "James, I need to be straight with you. Without proper identification or family contact, this becomes complicated. We need to verify your age, and if you're under eighteen—"

"I'm nineteen," James said quickly. "I told you, October 1977."

"But without ID, we can't confirm that. And hospital policy requires—"

A knock at the door interrupted her. Dr. Brennan appeared, looking tired but alert. "How's our patient this morning?"

"Awake and alert," Maria reported. "But we're having some documentation issues."

Rich glanced at James, then back to Maria. "I see. Well, let me examine him first, then we'll sort out the paperwork."

As Maria left, Rich moved to check James's hands, unwrapping the bandages carefully. "These look good," he said. "Much better than I expected. You're a lucky young man."

James watched Rich's face, trying to read his expression. "Am I... how long do I have to stay here?"

"Medically? You could probably go home this afternoon. The frostbite is superficial, your core temperature is normal." Rich rewrapped the bandages. "But there's the matter of where 'home' is for you."

James felt his chest tighten. "I can take care of myself."

"I'm sure you can. But hospital policy..." Rich sat down in the chair Maria had vacated. "James, there's someone here who's been asking about you. Someone who seems to care a great deal about what happens to you."

"Who?" But even as he asked, James knew.

"Callum Campbell. He says you know him?"

The memory of their conversation, of Callum's kindness, of the address he'd given him, came flooding back. But he hadn't been trying to reach Callum's house—he'd been looking for Anders's place on Brooke Street. The guilt hit him like a physical blow. Callum thought James had been coming to him for help.

"Is he here?" James asked, the guilt making his voice small.

"He's been here most of the night. Waiting to make sure you were okay." Rich studied James's face. "He seems to think you were trying to reach his house when this happened."

James looked down at his bandaged hands, shame burning in his chest. He'd been found like some pathetic stray, nearly frozen to death while looking for someone else entirely. And now Callum thought James had been seeking his help, had been trying to reach him. The kindness felt undeserved.

"Is he... can I see him?"

"That depends," Rich said carefully. "On whether you want to see him. And on what you want to do about your situation here."

James was quiet for a long moment. "What do you mean?"

"I mean you need somewhere to go when you're discharged. And from what I understand, Callum is offering that somewhere."

The offer he'd been too proud to accept just hours ago now felt like a lifeline. But accepting it meant admitting how desperate his situation really was, meant swallowing what little pride he had left.

"I can't prove who I am," James said quietly. "My wallet was in my backpack. It's probably buried somewhere in the snow."

Rich nodded. "We can work with that. Birth date, social security number, mother's maiden name—there are ways to verify identity without physical ID. The question is whether you're willing to let us help you."

James stared at the ceiling tiles, feeling the weight of the decision. Accept help and admit he had nothing, or maintain his pride and end up back on the streets.

"If I give you that information," he said slowly, "you won't contact my family?"

"Not unless you want us to."

James took a shaky breath. "Then yes. I want the help."

Rich smiled—the first genuine smile James had seen from anyone in weeks. "Good. Let me go get Callum. I think he's worn a hole in our waiting room floor."

Thirteen

*Sometimes salvation wears
the face of a stranger's care,
and home becomes the place
where someone says
you belong there.*

WHEN CALLUM WALKED into the hospital room, James was sitting up in bed, looking small and lost among the medical equipment. His bandaged hands rested awkwardly in his lap, and there were dark circles under his eyes that spoke of exhaustion deeper than one night's poor sleep.

"Hey," Callum said softly, unsure of the protocol for this situation. How do you greet someone you barely know who nearly died trying to reach safety?

"Hi." James's voice was barely above a whisper. "I'm sorry."

"Sorry?" Callum pulled the visitor's chair closer to the bed. "For what?"

"For this shit. For making you come here." James gestured at his bandaged hands, his voice raw. "I should've just... fuck, I should've gone with you."

Callum felt his chest tighten. "James, you have nothing to apologize for. Nothing."

They sat in awkward silence for a moment, both unsure how to navigate this new dynamic. Finally, Rich appeared in the doorway.

"Good news," he said, consulting his clipboard. "We've verified your identity through social security records. Everything checks out—you're free to go whenever you're ready."

James felt a rush of relief followed immediately by panic. Free to go where?

"The discharge nurse will go over care instructions for your hands," Rich continued. "Keep them dry, change the bandages twice daily, watch for signs of infection. You should be back to normal in a week or so."

"Thank you," James said, then looked at Callum uncertainly.

Callum cleared his throat. "James, my offer still stands. You're welcome to stay with me until you get back on your feet."

Pride and desperation warred in James's chest. "I can't just... you don't even know me, man."

"I know enough," Callum said simply. "I know you're a good person who's had some bad luck. And I know I have more space than I need."

James was quiet for a long moment, staring at his bandaged hands. Finally, he nodded. "Okay. Thank you."

The paperwork took another hour—forms to sign, insurance questions James couldn't answer, instructions about follow-up care. When they finally wheeled him to the hospital entrance, the storm was still raging, though not as fiercely as the night before.

"Jesus," Callum muttered, looking out at his snow-covered car. "I was hoping this would have let up by now."

As they made their slow way through the storm-battered streets, James pressed his face to the passenger window, scanning the snowdrifts along the sidewalks.

"What are you looking for?" Callum asked.

"My backpack. It has to be somewhere between the restaurant and where they found me." James's voice was tight with worry. "My wallet's in it. And... other things."

Callum could hear how important this was to him. "We'll find it. Once the storm passes, we'll retrace your route."

But James shook his head. "It could be buried under feet of snow by then. Everything I have left is in that bag."

Against his better judgment about driving in these conditions, Callum turned toward Old Louisville. "Show me where you think you might have dropped it."

They drove slowly through the empty streets, James pointing out landmarks he remembered from his desperate trek the night before. Near Brooke Street, they stopped and got out, Callum helping James search through snowdrifts while trying to protect his bandaged hands.

"There," James said suddenly, pointing to a dark shape barely visible under a mound of snow near an alley entrance.

Together, they dug out the frozen backpack, its straps stiff with ice. James clutched it against his chest with his forearms, unable to grip it properly with his injured hands.

"Got everything?" Callum asked, noting how James held the bag like it contained his life.

"Yeah. Everything." His voice cracked slightly on the word.

By the time they reached Callum's house, the afternoon light was already fading. The Victorian home looked warm and inviting with its glowing windows, though James noticed it was the only house on the block without any Christmas decorations.

Inside, Callum showed James to the guest room—a simply furnished space with a twin bed, small desk, and dresser. "Bathroom's right across the hall," he said. "Towels are in the closet."

James set his backpack carefully on the bed, finally able to unzip it with clumsy, bandaged fingers. Inside, everything was damp but intact—his wallet, a few changes of clothes, and wrapped carefully in a plastic bag, a small framed photograph.

Callum pretended not to notice as James quickly hid the photo in the desk drawer, respecting his privacy.

"I'll make us some dinner," Callum said. "Nothing fancy. Are you hungry?"

James realized he was starving—he couldn't remember his last real meal. "Yes, please."

Over soup and sandwiches, they talked carefully around the edges of their situation. Callum explained the house—how long he'd lived there, where things were, that James should make himself at home. James listened, still overwhelmed by the kindness of this near-stranger.

As evening settled over the house, Callum showed James how to work the deadbolt on his bedroom door.

"I want you to feel safe here," Callum said simply. "You can lock this anytime you want privacy or just need to know you're secure."

James nodded, touched by the gesture. That night, after Callum had gone to his own room, James did turn the lock—not because he didn't trust Callum, but because it had been so long since he'd had a door that was truly his to control.

Down the hall, Callum lay in his own bed, listening to the storm finally beginning to quiet outside. For the first time in months, the house didn't feel empty. There was someone else breathing within these walls, someone who needed the safety and warmth this place could provide.

As he drifted toward sleep, his mind wandered back over the past nine months—how he'd retreated from everything after Evan's death, how his friends had tried so hard to pull him back into the world. Maybe this was how healing actually happened—not by forgetting the past, but by finding new reasons to care about the future.

In the guest room, James lay awake longer, staring at the ceiling and thinking about the photograph hidden in the desk drawer. Two smiling faces from Halloween night, before everything fell apart. Before Ryan disappeared and James learned what it meant to be truly alone.

The first sign something was wrong came three days after Halloween, when James's rent check bounced.

He stared at the notice from his bank, reading it twice before the words sank in. Insufficient funds. But that was impossible—his parents had been depositing money into his account every month since he'd started college.

When he called the bank, the representative's voice was professionally sympathetic. "I'm sorry, Mr. McCarthy, but that account was closed by the primary account holder on November first."

Primary account holder. His father.

James hung up and immediately dialed home, his hands shaking as he waited for someone to answer. The phone rang and rang before going to the machine—his mother's careful voice asking callers to leave a message.

"Mom, it's James. Something's wrong with my bank account. Can you call me back? It's important."

He left three more messages over the next two days. No one called back.

By Friday, when his landlord knocked on his apartment door, James knew his world was collapsing.

"I'm sorry, son," Mr. Chen said, genuinely apologetic. "The check came back. I know you're a good kid, but I've got bills too."

"I can get the money," James said desperately. "There's been some mix-up with my account. My parents—"

"You've got until the fifteenth to make it right," Mr. Chen said gently. "After that, I have to start eviction proceedings."

The fifteenth. Two weeks.

James called Ryan immediately, but Ryan's phone rang straight through to voicemail too. Then he remembered—Ryan had said something about going home for the weekend, working things out with his parents.

That weekend stretched into a week with no word. James left message after message, growing more frantic with each one. Finally, on Thursday, his phone rang.

"James?" Ryan's voice sounded strange, distant.

"Ryan! Thank God. Where have you been? I've been trying to reach—"

"I can't talk long." Ryan sounded like he was in a public place, voices in the background. "I'm at a gas station payphone."

"A payphone? Why? What's going on?"

"My parents... they know, James. About us. About Halloween."

James felt the floor drop out from under him. "How?"

"Someone saw us. Someone from their church was at that hotel thing." Ryan's voice was barely audible. "They made me come home. They're... they're sending me to this church camp thing. To fix me."

"Fix you?" James didn't understand.

"I have to go. They're waiting in the car."

"When are you coming back?"

"I don't know. They say after Christmas, but..." Ryan's voice broke. "James, I'm so sorry. About everything."

The line went dead.

James stared at the phone in his hand, trying to process. Church camp. Fix him. The implications slowly sank in, each one worse than the last.

Two days later, the tuition bill for spring semester arrived—not to his parents' house as usual, but to his apartment. A note attached explained that per his request, all correspondence was now being sent to his new permanent address.

He'd never made such a request.

When he called the registrar's office, the woman on the phone was matter-of-fact. "We received the address change form along with a note that financial responsibility was being transferred to the student."

"But I didn't—"

"The form was signed by your father as the account holder. Is there a problem?"

James closed his eyes. "No. No problem."

The tuition bill was $4,200. His savings account—the $2,500 from summer jobs and weekend work—had been part of the same bank account his father closed. All of it, gone.

He had $42.38 in the old piggy bank he and Ryan kept for coffee money and late-night pizza runs. He'd counted every coin twice, frantically, hoping he'd somehow missed a twenty or miscounted the quarters. Looking at it spread across his desk, it seemed pathetic.

When he called home one more time, his mother finally answered.

"James." Her voice was cold, formal.

"Mom, please. I need to understand what's happening. The bank account, the tuition—"

"Your father and I have discussed this extensively with Father Morrison. We love you, but we cannot support choices that go against our faith and our values."

"Mom, I'm your son—"

"You will always be our son. But until you're ready to live according to God's plan for your life, we cannot enable behavior that puts your soul in jeopardy."

The line went dead.

James sat in his empty apartment, surrounded by furniture he couldn't afford to move and bills he couldn't pay, trying to understand how his life had imploded in less than two weeks.

The worst part wasn't the money or even the apartment. The worst part was the silence—from Ryan, from his family, from everyone who'd been part of his life just days before. It was as if Halloween night had erased him from existence, leaving behind only this hollow, frightened person who didn't know how to survive alone.

By November 15th, James had moved out of his apartment and into a sleeping bag on his friend Mike's floor. By Thanksgiving, Mike had gone home to his family, leaving James with keys to "apartment-sit" and a cupboard containing one can of Chef Boyardee.

He ate his Thanksgiving dinner alone, sitting on Mike's futon, trying not to think about the elaborate meal his family was probably sharing twenty minutes away in St. Matthews. Trying not to wonder if they'd set his place at the table or if they'd simply pretended he'd never existed.

When Mike returned, James had already lined up another couch to crash on, not wanting to overstay his welcome. The cycle continued through December—a few nights here, a few there, always apologetic, always temporary.

That's when he'd seen the "Now Hiring" sign at Wendy's and realized night shifts meant he could sleep in the back room if he was careful. It wasn't much, but it was something.

It was better than nothing.

It had to be.

Fourteen

≫⌐

In the morning light
of second chances,
two strangers
find familiar ground,
and discover that sometimes healing
is a treasure
meant to be found.

JAMES WOKE to the smell of coffee and something cooking downstairs. For a moment, he forgot where he was—the unfamiliar room, the clean sheets, the silence that came from being in a real house instead of a fast-food back room. Then memory flooded back, and with it, a mixture of gratitude and awkwardness.

His hands were still stiff and sore, the bandages making simple tasks difficult. Getting dressed took forever, and by the time he made his way downstairs, he could hear Callum moving around in the kitchen.

"Morning," Callum said, looking up from the stove. "How'd you sleep?"

"Good. Really good." James hovered in the doorway, unsure of the protocol. "Thanks."

"Eggs okay? I wasn't sure what you liked."

"Yeah, anything's fine." James sat at the small kitchen table, noticing a framed photograph stuck to the refrigerator with a magnet. Two men, arms around each other, smiling at the camera in what looked like a restaurant or bar.

Callum followed his gaze. "That's Evan," he said quietly, setting a plate of eggs and toast in front of James.

"He looks... nice." James studied the photo, seeing the easy happiness between the two men. "How'd you guys meet?"

Callum poured himself more coffee, settling into the chair across from James. "College, actually. Theatre 101 - I needed an elective and picked it randomly." He smiled at the memory. "Evan came in after class started, sat next to me, asked if he was late. Had this huge smile, this... energy."

He buttered a piece of toast for James, who was struggling with the bandages. "I was this serious farm kid, and he was this fearless little guy who didn't care who knew he was gay. Took me months to work up the courage to even talk to him properly."

"That must've been hard."

"It was. But once we got together, we found this whole little community. Other couples like us, friends who didn't judge. We'd have dinner parties, game nights." Callum's voice warmed at the memory. "Evan loved entertaining. He'd invite everyone over, cook these elaborate meals."

James thought about the Halloween party, Anders and his roommates. "I met some guys like that. At this party on Brooke Street."

Callum looked up, interested. "Halloween party? That sounds like Marcus and Trevor's place. And Anders, of course - he moved in with them last winter."

"You know Anders?"

"Not well, but yeah. He's been to some of our parties. Good guy. Been through a lot, though." Callum paused. "He mentioned he got kicked out by his family."

Callum looked down at his coffee. "Unfortunately, that happens to a lot of us. Or we just... get lost."

"Lost?"

"Sort of like a kid getting lost at an amusement park, only instead of going to the lost parent booth, there's no place for the kid to go. The parents, family, friends... they just run away. Don't even have the courage to say goodbye."

The words hit James like a physical blow. That was exactly what had happened to him—his family had simply erased him from their lives without warning, without explanation, without even the decency of a real goodbye.

Callum noticed James's reaction and realized what he'd said. "I'm sorry, I didn't mean—"

"No, it's... that's exactly what happened." James's voice was barely audible.

They sat in silence for a moment, both understanding passing between them.

"Anyway," Callum said gently, "we all try to help each other."

"They're like your new family," James said.

"Yes, you could call it that. We all need each other. And like any family, we don't always get along, but we love each other and we're there when it counts."

James nodded, processing this. The idea that there were people out there who chose to care for each other, who created their own families when their birth families failed them.

"Can I ask you something?" James said finally.

"Sure." Callum buttered another piece of toast for him.

"Are you gonna... decorate?"

The question seemed to come from nowhere. Callum blinked, realizing he hadn't given Christmas decorations a single thought. That had always been Evan's domain—he'd had the vision, the enthusiasm, the master plan. Callum had just followed directions: put the Santa here, string the lights there. But Evan was gone, and with him, the Christmas spirit.

"I... I hadn't really..."

James backed off immediately. "Sorry, I was just curious. Every other house has stuff up. Just wondered."

Inside, James was wishing he could have just one more Christmas that felt normal, that felt loved. He was probably on his own forever now, and the only thing he really wanted was to feel connected to something. Christmas seemed like... well, it was probably dumb.

"Never mind," James mumbled, slightly embarrassed. "It's probably just a stupid idea."

"No, it's not stupid at all," Callum said, reading his expression. "But I don't know what to do. That was Evan's role." His voice caught slightly on Evan's name.

"Could I... you think I could see your decorations? Sorry if that's too much..."

"No, it's okay. They're up in the attic and some are out in the garage. We can..." Callum got a little emotional.

"It's okay, Callum. I don't want to make you—"

"No, I think Evan would want me to... us to... decorate."

They spent the rest of the day going through boxes. Wreaths and light-up candles, Christmas stars and Santas, snowmen and snow globes, ivy and mistletoe and ornaments from around the world —one from each place Evan and Callum had traveled together.

The last one Callum pulled from the box was from Copenhagen, purchased just before Evan got sick. He stared at it, holding it as if it were a direct lifeline to Evan himself.

James watched this grown man handle a Christmas ornament with such tenderness, saw the tears in his eyes, and understood more about love and loss than he'd ever thought possible.

"Why don't you hang this one, James?"

"Oh, that's your special ornament, Callum. I couldn't..."

"Yes, you could. It helps me keep his memory alive, but I need to let go at the same time."

Standing back when the last ornament was hung, the decorations complete on the inside anyway, Callum admired the transformation of the house. It had a warmth throughout that he hadn't realized was lacking, so clouded had his soul been with grief.

James had almost forgotten himself during the decorating— listening to old Christmas music playing on Callum's CD player, baking slice-and-bake Pillsbury cookies, laughing when they hung mistletoe in completely wrong places. It felt like home. Like he actually had a home.

Both fought back emotion, both recognizing they were seeking the same thing, just at different points in their lives. Callum was learning to live again after loss, while James was learning what it meant to be truly cared for.

Outside, the snow continued to fall, but inside, surrounded by twinkling lights and the smell of sugar cookies, it felt like maybe Christmas was possible after all.

Maybe.

Fifteen

In the glow of memory's candle,
love becomes a living light,
and those we've lost
still guide us through
the darkness of the night.

"CAL, the boxes won't unpack themselves!" Evan's voice carried from the attic above, followed by the sound of footsteps and something heavy being dragged across the floor.

Callum looked up from his newspaper and sighed. It was barely December first, and already Evan was in full Christmas mode. "It's too early," he called back. "Thanksgiving was three days ago."

"It's never too early for Christmas!" Evan appeared at the top of the stairs, his hair dusted with cobwebs, carrying a box marked 'PARLOR TREE' in his careful handwriting. "Besides, we have the party in three weeks. Three weeks, Cal!"

Callum folded his paper with exaggerated resignation. "What's all this 'stuff' for, anyway? The house looks fine without it."

"Fine?" Evan nearly dropped the box. "Fine? Callum Campbell, this is not about 'fine.' This is about creating magic."

And it was magic, Callum had to admit, watching Evan transform their Victorian home into something from a fairy tale. Each year had a theme—sometimes Victorian elegance, sometimes winter wonderland, once memorably a "International Christmas" that had nearly driven them both to madness trying to coordinate decorations from seven different countries.

But Evan had his vision, and somehow it always worked. Each room got its own themed tree, its own decorations, and most importantly, its own lights. Evan's goal was ambitious: no electric lights in the house except what the trees, decorations, and fireplaces provided.

"I want it to feel like stepping back in time," Evan would explain to anyone who'd listen. "Like Christmas before electricity, when light meant something."

The only exception was the dining room chandelier, dimmed just enough to see the elaborate feast Evan would prepare for eighteen people—their chosen family, the friends who made Christmas Eve at Evan and Callum's house the event they looked forward to all year.

"Christmas Eve party? Are you insane?" people would ask, and Evan would grin wickedly while arranging place cards with military precision. "Honey, everyone else is stuck at boring family dinners pretending Uncle Harold isn't a racist again. We get all the good people who'd rather be with folks who actually like them!" He'd wink at Callum. "Besides, when you're already going to hell according to half your relatives, might as well throw a fabulous party on Jesus's birthday."

Callum grumbled about the early start, complained about hauling boxes, muttered about the expense of new ornaments Evan scouted year-round. But he did everything Evan asked, because watching his partner's face light up as each room came together was worth every minute of effort.

The centerpiece was always the parlor tree, visible through the front windows to anyone passing on St. James Court. Each year, they added the ornament from their latest trip—Venice, Paris, Dublin, Copenhagen. A growing collection of memories made manifest.

But the most important decoration wasn't on any tree. After every last ornament had been hung and every final detail was in place, Evan would perform his most sacred ritual. He'd take his great-grandmother's small white porcelain angel—his most prized possession—and place her on the parlor mantle. Then he'd light a single candle beside her, the final touch that completed their Christmas transformation. Only then would their home be ready for the guests who would arrive that evening.

"She watched over my great-grandmother through the Depression," Evan had told him that first Christmas. "Watched over my grandmother through the war. Watched over my mother until she died. Now she watches over us."

Callum had teased him about the superstition, but secretly loved the tradition. In that candlelit moment, with Evan's head on his shoulder and the angel keeping watch, everything felt complete.

Callum sat in the parlor, surrounded by the decorations he and James had put up the night before. The house was dark except for the tree lights spilling through the windows—still early morning, dawn barely breaking. He'd woken unable to sleep, pulled from bed by restless energy and the feeling that Evan's ghost was everywhere in these familiar decorations.

Everything in its place, just as Evan would have wanted. Except...

"Everything okay?"

James's voice from the doorway startled him. The young man stood in sweatpants and an old grey sweatshirt of Evan's that Callum hadn't been able to bring himself to donate.

The night before, Callum had gently asked if James had many clothes—not wanting to pry, but sensing James would never ask for help. Without waiting for an answer, he'd found the sweatpants and sweatshirt and simply handed them over before bed, disappearing before James could object or feel embarrassed. Maybe today, if the roads were passable, he'd take him out to pick up a few more things.

But for now, James was unaware of the significance of wearing Evan's old sweatshirt, and it took Callum a moment to shake Evan's memory upon seeing him in it.

"Yeah, I was just..." Callum's eyes found the empty spot on the mantle. Something was missing.

James followed his gaze. "Something wrong?"

Callum realized Evan's prized angel wasn't there. Unlike the other decorations, Evan never stored her with the Christmas boxes. During the off-season, she sat atop the glass curio cabinet in the music room, next to Evan's prized baby grand piano.

"We may both be hicks from the sticks," Evan used to joke with their friends, "but we're refined hicks."

"Hang on." Callum got up and walked past James, who followed curiously, bare feet padding softly on the hardwood floors, his sleepy eyes still adjusting to the house he was getting used to.

"Wow!" James stopped short in the doorway of the music room. They hadn't decorated this room, and he was taken aback by the piano dominating the space. This house was something else. His parents had a nice home, but this... this was something from an old movie. It felt like a home where New York society from the Gilded Age might feel comfortable, but it was also inviting, mysterious, asking to be explored.

Callum opened the glass cabinet and reached for the porcelain angel, still sitting where he'd left her months ago. As his fingers touched the delicate ceramic, it was as if he could feel Evan's energy, and he paused, closing his eyes and remembering the love of his life.

"She's really beautiful."

James's voice brought Callum back to the present.

"Yes, this was Evan's great-grandmother's. This was his most prized possession."

James's eyes widened. He was beginning to learn more about Evan from these little interludes—simple things that would take Callum somewhere else for a moment before bringing him back, often apologetic or misty-eyed, always carrying some sort of story.

"Let's go." Callum closed the cabinet and walked back to the front parlor. Placing the angel on the center of the mantle, he reached for a candle from the credenza behind and lit it, placing it in its holder as Evan had done for years, ever since their first Christmas together in the small apartment they'd shared.

The candle illuminated the porcelain in a warm yellow glow, flickering light across her face, along the wings and past the halo gently adorning her head. Callum resumed his seat on the sofa where James had found him. James sat on the other end, both staring up at the angel and the gentle light—the only source in the room aside from the window—sitting quietly in their thoughts, the flickering flame transporting them away from pain and into tranquility.

In the candlelit silence, two generations of loss found each other: Callum mourning the partner who'd made Christmas magical, and James discovering what home could feel like when someone cared enough to light a candle against the darkness.

Sixteen

When hope begins to bloom again
in winter's coldest hours,
love finds ways to plant new seeds
where sorrow once devoured.

THE PHONE RANG JUST as Callum was finishing his second cup of coffee. James had wandered off to explore the house, giving Callum a few moments alone with his thoughts and the lingering presence of Evan's angel watching from the mantle.

"Cal? It's Rich."

"Hey." Callum settled back in his kitchen chair. "Everything okay?"

"That's what I should be asking you. How's the kid doing? Hands healing okay?"

Callum glanced toward the hallway where he could hear

James's footsteps above. "He's... he's doing well. Better than I expected, honestly."

"And you? How are you holding up?"

There it was—the real reason for the call. Rich had been checking on him for months, along with Elena and David and the others, all of them walking on eggshells around his grief.

"I'm okay, Rich. Really."

"You sure? Because taking in a homeless teenager is... well, it's a big step. Especially for someone who's been..."

"Who's been what? Falling apart for nine months?"

Rich's silence confirmed it.

"I'm better," Callum said quietly. "Having James here... it helps. Gives me something to focus on besides missing Evan."

"Good. That's... that's really good, Cal. Just don't forget to take care of yourself too, okay?"

After Rich hung up, Callum sat listening to the sounds of James moving around upstairs. For the first time in months, his house felt alive.

James had found the family room, drawn by the afternoon light streaming through the bay windows. Unlike the formal parlor, this room felt lived-in—worn leather chairs, built-in bookshelves, and a coffee table covered with photo albums.

He shouldn't look. He knew that. These were private memories, not meant for a stranger's eyes. But the top album was open, displaying a photo of two men at what looked like a restaurant, both laughing at something off-camera. Callum looked younger, his face less shadowed by grief. The smaller man beside him—Evan —had his hand on Callum's arm, his eyes bright with mischief.

James carefully turned the page. More photos: the two men

on a beach somewhere, building sandcastles like children. At what looked like a birthday party, Evan blowing out candles while Callum watched with unmistakable adoration. A Christmas morning, both in pajamas, surrounded by wrapping paper and grinning like kids.

Then James found one that made him stop breathing. Someone had caught them in an unguarded moment—a quick kiss in what looked like their own kitchen, Evan standing on tiptoes to reach Callum's lips, both of them smiling into the kiss like they were sharing a secret.

James stared at the photo, his chest tight with something he couldn't name. He'd never seen anything like this—two men who looked... normal. Happy. In love the way straight couples were allowed to be in love.

When he and Ryan had kissed that first time, it had felt right in a way nothing else ever had. But being gay still felt underground to him, something that happened in shadowy bars or hidden corners. Something seedy and shameful, not something that looked like birthday parties and beach vacations and lazy Christmas mornings.

These photos showed something different. They showed what he'd been missing without knowing it existed.

"Finding anything interesting?"

James spun around, his face burning. "I'm sorry! I didn't mean to—"

"It's okay." Callum settled into the chair across from him. "I put those out there. If I didn't want them seen, I would've put them away."

"They're... you guys looked really happy."

"We were. For seventeen years, we really were."

James carefully closed the album. "I never saw anything like this before. Gay guys who just looked... I don't know, normal."

Callum studied his face. "What did you think we looked like?"

"I don't know. Different, I guess. Like the weird shit on TV or what they talk about at church." James's voice dropped. "Not like... not like, you know.. regular people just doing.. boring shit."

"We are regular people, James. That's all any of us are."

"We need to run some errands," Callum announced after lunch, jangling his keys. "Grocery store, maybe pick up some poinsettias. House needs a few things."

But twenty minutes later, they were pulling into the mall parking lot.

James felt his stomach clench. He'd spent countless afternoons here with friends from school, back when he had friends, back when his life was normal. "Why are we here?"

"I, uh..." Callum fumbled for an explanation. "I'm thinking of having my annual Christmas party again. Like Evan and I used to. Need to pick up some things for it."

James gave him a skeptical look but followed him inside, distracted by memories of walking these same corridors just months ago when everything was different.

In the department store, Callum began a performance worthy of an Oscar. "Oh, this is cute," he'd say, holding up a sweater. "If only they had it in my size. Looks like it would fit you, though."

Or: "I was going to get this for myself, but the color's all wrong. You should try it on."

After the fourth "coincidental" clothing discovery, James crossed his arms. "I know what you're doing."

"I have no idea what you mean."

"Callum."

He sighed. "Okay, look. If you don't want to accept my help, then consider it an early gift from Santa. I'll write up a list of what you owe me and you can pay me back later when you can, if that'll help ease your mind. But James... let me do this. It makes me feel... well, I can hear Evan now telling me to stop being an ass and help you."

James remembered the photos, the easy love between them, and his resistance crumbled. "Fine. But I'm paying you back."

"Deal."

Despite his discomfort, James found himself enjoying the process. The few clothes he'd managed to keep were worn and dirty, and after losing weight from barely eating, nothing fit right anymore. When Callum insisted on buying him a heavy winter coat to replace the one he'd nearly died in, James nearly cried.

"Were you serious?" James asked on the drive home, their bags in the backseat and the roads still treacherous with unplowed snow. "About the Christmas party?"

Callum was quiet for a moment. "It was mostly an excuse to buy you clothes."

"We should do it."

"What?"

"The party. We should have it." James's voice gained energy as he spoke. "Like the Halloween one I went to. Everyone coming together like... like a family. Like Anders said."

The more James talked, the more excited he became. What had started as a spark—a throwaway idea that Callum had used as a ruse—was becoming something bigger. The idea of having a family, of belonging somewhere after months of feeling thrown away, was more than he'd dared to imagine.

"James, I don't know..." Callum felt panic rising. "It's only a few days away. I'd have to call everyone and basically say, 'Hey, I know I've avoided you all since Evan died, but want to come to my Christmas party with this kid I just took in?'" He shook his head. "It's a lot to ask."

"But we already decorated," James pressed. "And you said Evan loved having everyone over. Maybe... maybe he'd want you to?"

Callum gripped the steering wheel tighter. It was a huge commitment. After months of pushing everyone away, of turning down every invitation and dodging every concerned phone call, he'd be opening his door—Evan's door—to all of them again. With James by his side, no less.

But looking at James's face, seeing how the idea was transforming him from the scared, defensive kid he'd met just days ago into someone with hope...

"The house isn't ready for eighteen people," Callum said weakly. "We'd need food, and the dining room needs more decorating, and—"

"I can help," James said quickly. "I want to help. Please, Callum. It could be like... like those pictures. Like what you and Evan had."

Callum pulled into their driveway and sat for a moment, engine running. This wasn't just about a party. This was about stepping back into life, into his community, into the world he'd shared with Evan. It was terrifying.

But James was practically vibrating with excitement, and Callum realized he couldn't disappoint him. Not when this was the first time he'd seen real hope in the kid's eyes.

"I'll call everyone," he said finally. "See if they have plans already. No promises, but..."

"Really?" James was practically bouncing in his seat.

"Really. But James, if people can't make it on such short notice—"

"They'll come," James said with startling confidence. "They're your family. They'll want to come."

Everyone Callum called had the same reaction. Initial worry—why was Callum calling?—followed by shock when he mentioned having Evan's party again.

"Cal, are you sure about this?" Elena asked carefully. "I mean, it's wonderful, but... it's only been nine months. Are you ready?"

David was more direct. "Who is this kid, exactly? Rich mentioned something about the hospital, but taking in a homeless teenager... that's a big step, especially right now."

Janet worried about the logistics. "Honey, Evan planned those parties for weeks. You're talking about Christmas Eve—that's three days away. What if people already have plans?"

But when Callum explained how James had lit up at the idea, how it seemed to give him hope after everything he'd been through, their concern shifted to cautious excitement.

"Evan would want this," Elena said finally. "He'd want his home filled with people again."

Rich was the easiest to convince, having seen James at the hospital. "If this kid is bringing you back to life, Cal, then hell yes, we'll be there."

After Callum hung up from each call, he could almost hear the secondary conversations starting. David immediately calling Elena: "Do you think he's okay? This seems sudden." Janet calling Rich: "Tell me more about this James. What exactly has Callum gotten himself into?"

Rich fielded most of the concerned follow-up calls. "Look,

I've seen them together. The kid's good for him. First time I've heard Callum sound like himself since the funeral."

By evening, the consensus was unanimous: if James was bringing Callum back from the grief that had consumed him for nine months, they were ready to welcome this boy with open arms. Evan's Christmas party would live again.

"Is Anders coming?" James asked over dinner, trying to sound casual but failing completely.

"Anders? You mean the trio on Brooke Street?"

"Yeah."

Callum studied James's face—the way he was pushing food around his plate, the slight flush in his cheeks. "I can call and invite them."

James tried to hide his smile, but Callum caught the spark in his eyes, the first real excitement he'd seen from the kid since he'd moved in.

"James," Callum said gently, "do you have feelings for Anders?"

"No!" The response was too quick, too defensive. "He just seemed nice, that's all. We talked, you know?"

Callum set down his fork. "It's okay if you do. There's nothing wrong with that."

"I don't know, alright?" James's teenage frustration came through, that inability to put complex feelings into words. "I don't know anything anymore. Everything's so fucked up and I can't... I don't know how to feel about anything."

"Hey, that's okay." Callum kept his voice calm. "You've been through hell, James. You nearly died a few days ago. You don't have to figure everything out right now."

James was quiet, still moving food around his plate.

"But," Callum continued carefully, "you've mentioned that Halloween conversation with Anders three times now. It obviously meant something to you."

"He told me about... like, how they all look out for each other," James said finally. "Like they're family, but not really family, you know? Just people who give a shit about each other. I'd never heard anyone talk like that before."

Callum nodded. He didn't know Anders well, but the kid seemed decent. Had his own baggage, his own story of family rejection that James might relate to. Maybe they could help each other.

"I'll give Anders a call," Callum said. "Invite him and Marcus and Trevor. See if they can make it."

"Really?" James looked up, hope flickering in his eyes again.

"Really. But James... just take things slow, okay? You're still healing. In a lot of ways."

James nodded, understanding more than he could articulate. "Thanks, Callum. For... for everything."

"Of course, James. It gives me.. well, I'm just happy to."

Later that evening, Callum dialed the number for the Brooke Street house.

"Hello?" Anders's voice was bright, curious.

"Anders? It's Callum Campbell."

"Oh! Hey, Callum. What's up?"

"Everything's fine. Actually, I'm calling with an invitation. I'm having Evan's Christmas Eve party this year, and I wanted to invite you and your roommates."

"No way! That's awesome! Marcus is taking off for Florida tomorrow night, but I can ask Trevor. When is it?"

"Christmas Eve, of course. Around seven."

"I'm totally there."

"Great. And Anders... there's someone here I think you might remember. James? You met him at your Halloween party."

"Wait, what? James? The kid with the Batman costume? He's with you? Whatever happened to him?"

"Yes, he's staying here," Callum said carefully. "Anders, James mentioned he talked with you at your Halloween party. Do you remember much about that night?"

"Oh shit, yeah. Actually, he came back to the house later that night, totally freaking out. Crying, couldn't even talk at first. His boyfriend.. uh, what was his name?... Ryan! He was chasing after him." Anders's voice grew serious. "Something bad happened at some hotel thing they went to. His dad caught them together or something. I sat with him on the porch, tried to calm him down."

"What happened after that?"

"They left together eventually. Ryan said he'd take him home, work things out. I figured they'd be okay, you know?" Anders paused. "Callum, what happened after that? Did they work it out?"

"His family cut him off completely. Bank account, tuition, everything. Ryan's parents sent him away."

"Jesus Christ." Anders was quiet for a moment. "When?"

"Right after that night. James has been homeless since November, Anders. Living on people's couches. He.. he, uh.. nearly died in that storm a few nights ago." Callum's voice quivered.

"Died! Fuck. I had no idea. Is he okay now? What happened? Oh my God, I should've.."

"He's fine, Anders.. at least he's safe now."

"I kept thinking maybe I'd see him around or something, but..." Anders's voice was heavy. "He's really okay?"

"Better. Physically healing. But he's been through hell, and I think seeing you might help. You were kind to him that night when he needed it."

"Of course I was kind to him. Kid was falling apart." Anders paused. "Does he... does he want to see me?"

"He specifically asked me to invite you. But Anders, he's in a really vulnerable place right now. That night at your house might be one of the last times he felt safe with someone who understood."

"I get it, Callum. I won't do anything to make it worse for him."

They talked for a few more minutes about how Anders might help, his promises that he'd be cool, offers to bring food or help with stuff.

"I think James might enjoy seeing you sooner than later, but I won't say anything," Callum said finally.

"Could I surprise him tomorrow, if that's cool?"

"We'll be out getting things for the party. Why don't you plan to have dinner with us, if you're free?"

"Yeah, totally. I hadn't planned anything here anyway."

"How are you doing, really?" Callum asked, remembering Anders talking with him shortly after he'd first arrived in Louisville. It hadn't even been a year, just a few months before Evan died.

Anders was quiet for a moment. "It's my first Christmas since getting kicked out. I'll be okay though."

"I know you will be. But how are you right now?"

"It's... kinda shitty, honestly."

Callum knew. He knew exactly.

"Let's have that dinner then. Nothing fancy. Why don't you... no, better yet, we'll come get you. I won't tell James. It'll be a surprise."

"Oh man, that'll be awesome!" Anders's voice perked up considerably.

"We'll drive by at six then. We can head over to Bardstown Road."

"Dude, James is gonna flip!"

"He will. But Anders..."

"Yeah?"

"Let's take everything a day at a time. I know it's cliche, and I'm telling myself that too."

"Shit, I'm sorry, Callum. I should've asked... how are you doing? Since..."

"I have my moments. James found Evan's photo album today. Made me smile, seeing how he looked through the photos. Told me he'd never seen 'gay guys' like that."

Anders laughed. "He's got a lot to learn, right?"

"We all do."

"See you tomorrow."

"Looking forward to it. I..."

"What?"

"Nah, it's nothing."

"Come on, spit it out."

"Christmas kinda blows, you know?"

Callum did know. Very well.

"Yeah. But James wants to keep Evan's party thing going, so maybe it won't suck as much." He said it more for himself than Anders, but it felt true.

"It's gonna be fun."

"It will be."

"Callum?"

"Yeah?"

"Thanks for calling me. It really... helped."

❄

Later that evening, Callum stopped by James's bedroom door. "Spoke with Anders. He's definitely coming, and he'll ask Trevor, but Marcus is heading to Florida."

James stood in his doorway, fidgeting with the hem of his new sweatshirt. Finally, he blurted out: "The night I was walking in the storm... I was trying to get to Anders's place. Not yours."

Callum paused, processing this. "That makes sense, actually. Given everything you've been telling me."

"I'm sorry. I feel guilty—"

"Nothing to be sorry about, James. It changes nothing for me. I still would've come to get you regardless."

"Really?"

"Of course. I don't have conditions on... well, on caring about you. I'm always here for you. You're sort of like my..." He paused, thinking. "Well, I'm not old enough to be your dad—"

"You're nothing like my dad," James interrupted.

"And I'm too old to be... well, you know what I mean." They both did. "You're sort of like my kid brother, I guess. And I love you like that, if that makes sense."

"You love me?"

"Like a kid brother, yeah. Is that... is that too much?"

James's eyes filled with tears—months of pain and loneliness and fear finally having somewhere to go. He hadn't felt loved since Halloween, since his whole world fell apart.

Callum immediately worried he'd said something wrong, but he held James nonetheless, apologizing, reassuring.

When James finally calmed down, he managed: "I love you too. As my big brother."

They both snickered through their tears.

"Best get to bed," Callum said. "We've got work to do for the party. Only two days until you see your cute Anders."

James blushed, wiping his eyes. "He's just a friend."

"I know, I know. And I like him too. Not in that way, but you know what I mean."

"Go to bed!" James laughed, embarrassed and eager to stop crying. But his heart was warm. "Goodnight, big bro."

"Goodnight, little bro."

Seventeen

The wounds we carry
teach us how to recognize another's pain,
and in the sharing of our scars
we learn to love
and heal again.

ANDERS HUNG up the phone and sat in the silence of the Brooke Street house. Marcus had been packing for his Florida trip all evening and had finally gone to bed, Trevor was out somewhere, and the quiet pressed in around him like a familiar weight.

James. That scared kid from Halloween, the one who'd cried in his arms on the front porch just two months ago, had been homeless this whole time. Had nearly died in that storm.

Anders closed his eyes and felt his chest tighten with recognition. He knew exactly what James had been going through because he'd lived it himself, just eleven months ago. The age difference between them—five years—felt meaningless when it came to that particular kind of pain. Getting thrown away by family hurt just as much at twenty-five as it did at nineteen.

Maybe more, because at twenty-five, you thought you were supposed to have your shit together.

Anders had been so careful. Four years of art school in Chicago, living with his boyfriend Patrick in their tiny studio apartment, keeping his worlds completely separate. His parents thought Patrick was his roommate, nothing more. They'd send care packages and call every Sunday, and Anders would edit his life into acceptable pieces—school projects, part-time job, the weather.

But graduation changed everything. His parents insisted on coming to the ceremony, wanted to take him and Patrick to dinner afterward to celebrate. "We're so proud of you, honey," his mother had said over the phone. "Our son, the artist!"

Patrick had been nervous about it, but Anders convinced him it would be fine. One dinner. They'd be careful, keep their hands to themselves, play the roommate game they'd perfected.

Everything went wrong in the span of thirty seconds.

They'd all gone back to the apartment afterward—his parents wanting to see where their son lived, talking about helping him pack for the move back home while he figured out his next steps. Patrick was in the tiny kitchen making coffee, and Anders was showing his father some of his final projects when his dad stopped mid-sentence.

Above their bed, barely visible from the living area, hung a small framed photo they'd forgotten about. Anders and Patrick at the Art Institute, Patrick's arms around Anders from behind, both of them laughing, clearly more than friends.

His father's face went through a series of expressions—confusion, understanding, then something Anders had never seen before. Disgust. Rage.

"Get your things," his father said quietly. "We're leaving. Now."

"Dad, let me explain—"

"I said get your things. You're coming home with us."

"No." The word came out before Anders could stop it. "I'm not going anywhere."

That's when his father hit him. Not a slap, but a full punch to the face that sent Anders stumbling backward into their bookshelf. Patrick dropped the coffee mugs, the crash making Anders's mother scream.

"You are not my son," his father said, advancing on him. "No son of mine would choose to be a fucking faggot."

The next few minutes were a blur of violence and shouting. His father's fists, his mother crying, Patrick trying to intervene and getting shoved hard into the wall. By the time it was over, Anders had a broken rib, a split lip, and bruises blooming across his face and chest. His parents had left, taking their pride and their love with them.

Anders spent that first night in a hospital emergency room, lying about how he'd gotten his injuries, getting his ribs X-rayed and wrapped. Patrick, shaking and traumatized by what he'd witnessed, could barely look at him.

"Maybe you should go home," Patrick whispered, cleaning blood from Anders's face with a dishrag. "Work things out with them."

"There's nothing to work out, Pat. You heard what he said."

But Anders could already feel Patrick slipping away. Over the next few days, his boyfriend grew distant, uncomfortable, as if Anders had somehow become the reason their quiet life had exploded into violence and chaos. When the silence between them became unbearable, Anders reached out to the one person who might understand.

He'd known Marcus for about a year—they'd met at a bar in Boystown when Marcus was visiting Chicago, hitting it off immediately as friends who got each other's jokes. Marcus lived in Louisville with his roommate Trevor, two guys who'd been roommates since college and simply kept the arrangement going after graduation. They both had boyfriends, split expenses, enjoyed each other's company while knowing when to give each other space. It worked.

Anders and Patrick had even visited once, with Marcus and Trevor taking them to The Connection, a gay bar with a great dance floor and drag review. It had been a good weekend—easy, comfortable, the kind of friendship Anders had always wanted but never quite found in Chicago.

Now, desperate and hurting, Anders found himself dialing Marcus's number to share what had happened and ask his thoughts about Patrick being... well, weird.

"Pat's ready to run when things get tough," Marcus said bluntly. "Why don't you come down and stay here for the holidays? We've got room. We can move Trevor's shit out of that little office upstairs, put in a futon, and voilà—instant Anders guest room!"

Marcus's prediction proved accurate. Within a day of that call, Patrick asked Anders to move out. "I can't handle this," he said, unable to meet Anders's eyes. "I'm sorry, but I can't."

What Marcus had offered as a New Year's Eve visit became Anders's permanent escape from a life that had disintegrated in the span of thirty seconds.

The move south was a blur of borrowed money for bus tickets and sleepless nights in Marcus and Trevor's guest room, crying into pillows that smelled like unfamiliar fabric softener. While his ribs healed, Anders wrestled with guilt about eating their food, using their utilities, taking up space in their lives without being able to contribute anything in return.

"Stop being an idiot," Trevor told him one night, finding Anders washing dishes at 2 AM because sleep wouldn't come. "We've all been where you are. Marcus got kicked out at seventeen. I lived in my car for three months after college when my family found out about my ex. This is what we do—we take care of each other."

Gradually, the Louisville gay community wrapped around Anders like a warm coat. Friends of Marcus and Trevor brought clothes that actually fit, helped him find part-time work at a local gallery, and included him in dinner parties and game nights and lazy Sunday brunches. They didn't treat him like charity—they made him family.

That's how he met Evan and Callum.

It was at one of Elena and David's dinner parties, perhaps six weeks after his arrival in Louisville. Anders was still raw then, still jumping at loud noises and flinching when voices were raised. Evan must have noticed him sitting alone on the back porch, picking at his food and trying to disappear.

"Mind if I sit?" Evan had asked, settling beside him without waiting for an answer. He was small and fierce-looking, but something gentle lived in his eyes. "You look like someone who needs a friend."

They'd talked for hours. Evan told him about his own family—the white trash background he'd escaped, the brothers who'd beaten him up more times than he could count before he got smart and got out. He talked about finding love with Callum, building a chosen family in Louisville, creating a life that was fully his own.

"Honey, let me tell you something," Evan had said as the party wound down around them, his voice carrying that familiar mix of sass and wisdom despite the weariness Anders could see in his thin face. "You need to accept the help. Accept the love. Everyone here has their own sob story about getting cast aside or beaten down, but guess what? We've got each other now, and that's not just something—that's everything."

He'd looked directly at Anders then, those sharp eyes still fierce even as his body seemed more fragile than it should. "Like it or not, sugar, you're stuck with us now. And someday, you'll be the one helping someone else, because Lord knows people are still gonna need our support. Our laughter and love and occasional dramatic crying fits."

Evan had paused, studying Anders's still-healing face with a knowing look. "Being gay isn't just about who you're sleeping with, darling. It's about recognizing your responsibility—to yourself and to each other. We're all we've got, so we better damn well take care of our own."

Just over a month later, Anders sat in the back of a funeral home, watching that same community rally around Callum, who looked like his soul had been buried with Evan. No church would host the service—not that Evan would've wanted one anyway—but the funeral home was packed with people whose lives Evan had touched.

Anders cried for Evan, but also for the brutal clarity of understanding what he'd been given. This was his family now. This was his home. The people in these uncomfortable folding chairs, mourning together, supporting Callum through the unthinkable—these were his people.

Back home didn't exist anymore. It never really had.

Sitting alone in the Brooke Street house, Anders wiped his eyes and laughed softly, remembering Evan's voice: "Shed the tears and get it out of your system, girl, because we've got things to do and people to see!"

God, he didn't know how Callum had done it—made it through all these months without Evan. No wonder he'd helped James. He needed to, just like everyone in their community needed to help when they could. And James needed it, desperately, just like Anders had needed it eleven months ago.

Tomorrow, he'd see James again. He'd hug that kid and tell him what Evan had told him—that he was home now, that he was family, that the worst was behind him.

It was Christmas, after all. Time for miracles, even small ones.

Especially small ones.

Eighteen

In the warmth of unexpected friendship,
two hearts
begin to understand
that healing happens in the spaces
where someone takes your hand.

"WHERE ARE WE GOING?" James asked as Callum turned onto Brooke Street. The familiar Victorian houses looked different in the evening light, their Christmas decorations twinkling against the snow.

"Just picking someone up," Callum said, trying to hide his smile as he pulled up in front of the house James recognized from Halloween night.

James felt his stomach flip. "We're not going to—"

Before he could finish, the front door flew open and Anders came running out into the cold, his breath visible in puffs as he jogged toward their car, pulling on his coat as he came.

"Hey!" Anders called out, yanking open the back door and sliding in with a rush of cold air. "Sorry, hope you don't mind me tagging along."

James spun around in his seat, his face transforming from confusion to pure joy. "Anders! Holy shit, what are you doing here?"

"Callum called and said you might not mind some company for dinner," Anders said, settling into the backseat and immediately bringing his upbeat energy into the car. "Plus, I figured someone needs to make sure you two don't just sit around being all serious and grown-up."

"Are you kidding? This is fucking awesome!" James was practically bouncing in his seat, more animated than Callum had seen him since the hospital.

"So did you miss me?" Anders asked with exaggerated drama, batting his eyelashes. "Tell me you pined away thinking about our deep philosophical conversation on my porch."

James laughed, the sound bright and genuine. "Yeah, actually I did. That was... that night was important to me."

Anders's joking tone softened. "Hey, I hope you don't mind, but Callum filled me in a little bit on what happened after that. How you holding up?"

James flinched slightly at the directness of the question, but something in his expression showed he was touched that Anders even asked. Like he actually cared.

"Better," James said quietly. "Way better than I was."

The drive to Bardstown Road was filled with Anders catching James up on what he'd been doing—his job at the gallery, funny stories about Trevor's latest boyfriend drama, anything to keep the mood light. Callum listened, remembering how Evan used to do the same thing, filling any silence with chatter and laughter.

When they pulled up to Molly Malone's, James looked at the cozy Irish pub with its warm lights spilling onto the sidewalk. "This place looks cool."

"Evan loved their fish and chips," Callum said quietly. "Said it was the closest thing to decent pub food in Louisville." There was something in his voice that suggested this place held memories.

They made their way inside, and Callum was relieved when the hostess led them to their usual corner booth without him having to ask. The familiar worn wood and dim lighting felt like a hug from an old friend.

"Man, this is perfect," James said, sliding into the booth. "I haven't been anywhere like this since..." He trailed off, realizing he was about to mention his old life.

"Since when?" Anders asked gently, settling across from him.

"Just since before everything went to shit," James said, his teenage bluntness cutting through any attempt at delicate conversation.

Callum took the seat next to James, studying the menu he knew by heart. "Well, tonight's about making better memories."

"Exactly!" Anders said with deliberate cheer. "Besides, I have a feeling tomorrow night's going to be either amazing or a complete disaster."

"Probably both," Callum admitted, and they all laughed.

The server came by, and after they'd ordered, Anders turned his full attention to James. "Okay, but seriously, how are you doing? And don't give me some bullshit answer—I mean really, how are you?"

James held up his bandaged hands, wiggling his fingers slightly. "Better. Way better than a few days ago. The hands are healing up good, and..." He paused, looking between Anders and

Callum. "I don't know, I feel like maybe I'm not gonna die, you know? Like maybe things might be okay."

"That's huge, man," Anders said, and James could hear genuine relief in his voice. "When Callum told me what happened to you... fuck, James, I was so worried. I kept thinking about that night at my house, how messed up you were, and then you just disappeared."

"Yeah, well, turns out getting disowned by your family really fucks up your holiday plans," James said with bitter humor.

Callum reached over and squeezed James's shoulder. "You're not disappearing again. Not on my watch."

"Or mine," Anders added, and something in his tone made James look at him more carefully.

They talked about lighter things while they waited for food —Anders telling stories about the gallery, James describing his new room at Callum's house, Callum sharing memories of past Christmas parties that made Evan sound like a cross between Martha Stewart and a Broadway director.

"He once spent three hours arranging place cards," Callum said, shaking his head. "Three hours. For eighteen people. He had this whole system about who should sit next to whom to create the best conversations."

"Sounds like he knew what he was doing though," Anders said. "I heard people talking about those parties - they sound amazing."

"They were," Callum agreed, and James noticed how his voice got softer when he talked about Evan. "I have no idea how to live up to that."

"You don't have to be him," James said quietly. "Just... I don't know, do what feels right to you."

Both Anders and Callum looked at him with surprise, and James blushed. "I mean, that's what you keep telling me, right?

That I can't go back to who I was before, but I can figure out... whatever comes next?"

"Kid's got a point," Anders said, grinning. "Look at you, being all wise and shit."

When their food arrived, the conversation drifted to tomorrow's party preparations, but eventually James brought up the question that had been haunting him.

"I keep thinking about Ryan," he said quietly, picking at his burger. "He called me once, like a week after Halloween. From a payphone at some gas station. Said his parents were sending him to church camp to fix him." James's voice was small, uncertain. "I didn't really get what that meant. Fix what?"

Anders set down his fork and leaned forward. "James, do you know what conversion therapy is?"

James shook his head, but something cold was settling in his chest.

"It's torture," Anders said bluntly, his usual upbeat tone completely gone. "They try to shame you, scare you, make you hate yourself so much you'll pretend to be straight just to make the pain stop. They call it 'fixing' you because they think being gay is some kind of disease." His hands were clenched on the table. "It's fucking evil, and it doesn't work. It just breaks people."

"What do you mean?" James whispered.

"I mean they'll do whatever it takes to try to change who Ryan is," Callum added quietly. "Humiliation, isolation, making him think God hates him. Sometimes worse."

James went very quiet, his food forgotten. "You mean Ryan is... they're trying to make him not gay anymore?"

"If that's what they're calling it, then yeah, probably," Anders said, hearing his tone and trying to take it down a notch.

"But that's..." James's voice cracked, and his hands started shaking. "That's so fucking evil. How can people think that's okay? How can they be so cruel to their own kid?"

His voice was rising, and other diners were starting to look over. Callum put a steadying hand on James's arm.

"Let's try and not get too upset," he said softly. "But you're not wrong to be angry."

"I just..." James's eyes filled with tears. "Ryan was so sweet, you know? He was the first person who made me feel like.. like he really liked me... And now they're trying to torture him into being someone else?" He wiped his eyes with the back of his unbandaged hand. "You don't think my parents would've done that to me, do you?"

"I don't know, kid," Callum said honestly. "But they can't hurt you now."

Anders, without thinking, reached across the table and rested his hand on James's wrist, just below the bandages. "Hey, you're safe now. We're not going to let anything happen to you."

James looked down at Anders's hand on his, and something shifted in his expression. The touch was gentle, reassuring, but James felt something else too—a flutter of awareness that made his cheeks warm.

Callum noticed the moment, saw the way James's breathing changed slightly, the way he didn't pull his hand away. He said nothing, just smiled slightly and moved the conversation forward.

"So what are you doing for Christmas Day, Anders?" he asked, changing the subject. "Any plans?"

Anders reluctantly moved his hand back, but his eyes stayed on James's face. "Not really. Trevor's going to his boyfriend's family thing, and Marcus is still in Florida. So it's just me and whatever's on TV, I guess."

James suddenly looked stricken, his attention snapping away from the lingering warmth where Anders had touched him. "Oh shit. I don't... I don't have any presents. For anyone. And..." He trailed off, looking miserable. "God, I've gotta' figure out how to..."

"James, you don't need to buy presents," Anders said firmly. "You know that's not what makes Christmas good, anyway."

"I know, but..." James tapped his head, frustrated. "It's like I can't even have Christmas, you know? I keep thinking about how it used to... I can't even buy anyone a stupid gift." His voice got smaller. "It's like.. I lost everything."

"You've got yourself," Callum said quietly. "And I'm sure everyone will be happy just to get to know you."

"But it's not the same," James insisted, his teenage frustration bleeding through. "It's supposed to be special, and I'm just gonna be this charity case who shows up empty-handed."

"You're not a charity case," Anders said with more heat than he'd intended. "Don't ever call yourself that. You think I had presents last year after my dad beat the shit out of me and threw me out? You think any of us did the first Christmas after our families decided we weren't worth loving anymore?"

The table went quiet. Anders took a breath, visibly collecting himself.

"I'm Sorry. I just... it pisses me off when you talk about yourself like that. You're really a special guy and I..."

Callum caught Anders's eye and winked—a gesture that made Anders smile despite his anger. There was something knowing in that wink, some secret that James wasn't part of yet.

"Well," Callum said carefully, once again redirecting the conversation, "we've got nothing fancy planned. To be honest, I'm still surprised we're doing the party tomorrow night," he laughed. "Why don't you come over for Christmas Day, Anders? No sense in you being alone."

Anders brightened immediately, his natural optimism reasserting itself. "Really? You sure you don't mind?"

"That'd be awesome," James said quickly, then blushed at how eager he sounded.

"Then it's settled," Callum said. "Though I should warn you, I have no idea what we're doing for Christmas dinner. Evan always handled that."

"I can cook," Anders offered. "Nothing fancy. I can make a mean breakfast, but I bet between the three of us we can figure out something for dinner."

"See?" Callum smiled. "Already working out better than I expected."

James was looking between them, still seeming a little melancholy despite the plans. Callum could tell he was struggling with something deeper than just presents—the loss of all his childhood Christmas traditions, the family gatherings he'd never have again.

Anders seemed to sense it too. "You know," he said thoughtfully, "maybe we should make our own traditions this year. Do Christmas our way."

"What do you mean?" James asked.

"I mean, fuck what Christmas is supposed to look like. What do *we* actually want Christmas to be?"

James thought about it. "I don't know. Warm, I guess. And... safe. Like nobody's gonna judge you or try to change you or throw you out."

"That sounds perfect," Callum said softly, thinking about how Evan would have loved this conversation.

"Okay, but first we have to survive tomorrow's party," Anders said, deliberately lightening the mood. "Speaking of which, Callum do you need any help?"

"Oh, right!" Callum straightened up, putting on an theatrical air of importance. "I'm placing you in charge of entertainment, Anders."

"Me? I don't know anything about party games."

"That's why James is going to help you," Callum added with a gesture like he was knighting them at Buckingham Palace. "You two are officially the social committee!"

"Me?" James looked surprised but pleased. "What do I know about entertaining people?"

"You surely know how to have fun," Callum said. "And you know what it's like to need people to be kind to you. What else is there?"

"Okay, so what kind of games are we talking about?" Anders asked, pulling out a napkin and pen from his jacket pocket. "I mean, these are adults, right? We can't just do Pin the Tail on the Donkey."

"Why not?" James asked. "That could be hilarious with a bunch of drunks!"

"Ooh, good point. Okay, write that down." Callum laughed and watched them go off to the races.

As dessert arrived, James and Anders began brainstorming in earnest, their ideas growing more outlandish and ridiculous with each suggestion. Soon they were both laughing, building off each other's creativity, completely absorbed in their planning.

"What about charades, but only with bad Christmas movies?" James suggested.

"Yes! But everyone has to act out the whole movie in like thirty seconds," Anders added.

"Or we could do that thing where you write down weird phrases and people have to draw them?"

"Pictionary! But Christmas Pictionary. With bonus points if you can make it dirty!"

Callum watched them, occasionally contributing an idea but mostly just observing. Their energy was infectious, the way they sparked off each other, how Anders's natural enthusiasm brought out James's playful side while James's earnestness kept Anders grounded.

He could almost see Evan sitting there beside him, taking over the conversation and having everyone in stitches with his commentary. But instead of the usual sharp pain that came with thoughts of Evan, Callum felt something warmer. He could imagine Evan watching these two with the same affection Callum felt, seeing the healing happening between them.

"What about music?" James was saying. "Could we do some kind of music game?"

"Oh, definitely. Christmas song trivia? Or that game where someone hums a song and everyone has to guess?"

"That could get ugly fast," Callum laughed. "Half our friends can't carry a tune in a bucket, but think they're Mariah."

"Even better!" Anders grinned. "More embarrassing, more fun."

As they talked and planned, Callum found himself studying their faces—Anders with his determined cheerfulness that couldn't quite hide the sadness underneath, and James with his raw honesty that made everything he felt visible in his expression. Two young men who'd been hurt by the people who were supposed to love them, now finding joy in planning a party for a community that actually would.

Callum found himself actually looking forward to tomorrow's party. Not just enduring it for James's sake, but anticipating it. Evan had always said the best parties were the ones where people felt free to be themselves, where laughter came easily and nobody had to pretend to be someone they weren't.

Watching James and Anders laugh together, seeing the light come back into both their faces, Callum understood something Evan had tried to tell him so many times: sometimes the best way to heal your own heart is to help heal another's.

And sometimes, if you're very lucky, you get to watch two wounded souls find each other.

And remember what joy feels like.

Nineteen

~~

A room full of strangers
with hearts open wide,
became the family
that welcomed him inside.

CALLUM STOOD IN HIS KITCHEN, watching James and Anders through the window as they hung string lights around the back porch. Their laughter carried through the glass —genuine, easy laughter that made something in his chest loosen. James was holding the ladder while Anders climbed, both of them arguing good-naturedly about whether the lights were even.

It had been like this all afternoon. The boys had thrown themselves into party preparation with the intensity of kids building a fort, transforming the house with an energy Callum hadn't felt since... well, since Evan's last party. But this felt different somehow. Where Evan had orchestrated every detail with military precision, James and Anders approached it like a grand adventure, improvising solutions and finding joy in the chaos.

"Does this look right?" James called up to Anders, who was now precariously balanced on the top step, trying to drape lights over the porch overhang.

"If by 'right' you mean 'like a drunk electrician did it,' then yeah, perfect," Anders called back.

James laughed—that full-bodied laugh Callum was still getting used to hearing. Three days ago, the kid had been barely speaking above a whisper. Now he was bantering with Anders like they'd known each other for years.

The doorbell rang, and Callum's stomach clenched. They were early. He'd hoped for a few more minutes to prepare himself, to figure out how to introduce James without making it weird, how to explain what the kid meant to him when he wasn't entirely sure himself.

He opened the door to find Rich and his partner Wynn on the porch, both carrying covered dishes and wearing identical expressions of barely contained curiosity.

"Cal," Rich said, pulling him into a quick hug. "Place looks great."

Wynn, a thin man with kind eyes and prematurely grey hair, kissed Callum's cheek. "We brought the spinach artichoke dip you always liked. Though I made extra because Rich said there might be more people than usual?"

"Yeah, about that..." Callum started, then stopped as James and Anders appeared in the hallway, both slightly out of breath from their decorating efforts.

Rich's face lit up immediately when he saw James. "There he is! James, how are you feeling?" His medical training kicked in automatically as he took in James's appearance—the color in his cheeks, the way he moved without favoring his hands.

grandfather had dressed up as the Virgin Mary for the nativity play.

"He trusts you," Rich continued quietly. "More than that, he's letting himself care about people again. About Anders, obviously, but also about you."

"I don't know what I'm doing, Rich. Half the time I feel like I'm going to screw this up."

"You won't." Rich's voice carried the confidence of years of friendship. "You know why? Because you're not trying to fix him. You're just... letting him be safe."

Elena finished her performance to enthusiastic applause, and Anders jumped up next. His memory, it turned out, involved a disastrous Christmas morning when he was twelve and had tried to make breakfast for his little sister while their parents nursed hangovers. The performance involved a lot of smoke effects (provided by waving his hands dramatically) and ended with him lying flat on the floor to represent passing out from smoke inhalation.

"The best part," he said, still lying on the carpet, "was that my sister thought I was the greatest big brother ever. Even though I nearly burned the house down, she got to eat ice cream for breakfast while the fire department aired out the kitchen."

The laughter that followed was warm and inclusive, the kind that invited you in rather than leaving you out. James was laughing too, that full-body laugh that made his whole face light up.

When it was James's turn, Callum tensed. What happy Christmas memory could the kid possibly have? His family had thrown him out, he'd been on his own for months...

But James stood up with only a slight tremor in his hands. "Mine's recent," he said. "Like, really recent."

He walked over to the Christmas tree and touched one of the ornaments—a simple glass ball that caught the light.

"Christmas morning!" David called out.

James shook his head, still touching the ornament gently.

"Opening presents?" Sarah guessed.

Again, James shook his head, but he smiled encouragingly and gestured for them to keep trying.

"Shopping for ornaments?" Elena suggested.

James moved his hands in a hanging motion, then stepped back to admire the tree.

"Decorating!" Tom called out. "Decorating the tree!"

James pointed at him with both hands, grinning. "Bingo!" Then his expression grew more serious.

"Two nights ago," he said, "I helped decorate this tree. And for the first time in... I don't know, maybe ever... I felt like I was part of something. Like I belonged somewhere."

He looked directly at Callum, his voice barely above a whisper. "I know it sounds stupid, hanging... hanging fucking ornaments." His eyes widened as the profanity slipped out. "Sorry, I'm sorry, I didn't mean to—"

But Anders was already moving toward him, gently placing a hand on his shoulder. "It's okay," Anders said quietly. "You're okay."

James took a shaky breath and continued, his voice trembling. "Callum kept asking where I thought... where I thought things should go. Like what I said mattered, you know? No one ever..." He stopped, swallowing hard. "And when we were done, he made hot chocolate and we just sat there, and I..."

A tear rolled down his cheek and his voice broke completely. "I thought... I thought maybe..." He choked on the words, unable to get them out.

Anders squeezed his shoulder gently. "Take your time."

James wiped his face with the back of his hand, voice barely a whisper. "Maybe this is what... what it's supposed to feel like. Having a home."

The room was absolutely silent. James's cheeks were red, but he kept going, his voice getting stronger.

"The memory I want to act out is that feeling. Of belonging somewhere."

He walked to Elena first. "Elena," he said softly, touching her shoulder. She smiled and nodded encouragingly. Then to Rich. "Dr. Brennan—I mean, Rich." Then to Wynn. "Wynn." To Sarah. "Sarah." To David. "David." He paused at Tom, uncertain.

"Tom," Tom said gently.

"Tom." James touched his shoulder. Then to Janet. "Janet."

At first, people weren't sure what he was doing—some exchanged glances, confused. But after the third person, understanding dawned across their faces. Eyes began darting between each other as they realized what they were witnessing.

James came back to the center and spread his arms wide, like he was embracing all of them at once.

"Family," he said simply, his voice breaking on the word.

There wasn't a dry eye in the room.

Elena was the first to move, pulling James into a fierce hug. "Sweet boy," she murmured. "Of course you belong here."

Then everyone was hugging him—this kid they'd barely met, but who had somehow become one of them in the space of a single evening. Rich clapped him on the back, Wynn kissed his forehead, Janet reached for his hands without thinking and squeezed them tight.

"Ow!" James yelped involuntarily.

Janet immediately dropped his hands, her face going pale. "Oh God, I'm so sorry! Your hands, I forgot—I'm such an idiot—"

"No, no, it's okay," James said quickly, flexing his fingers. "Really, I'm fine."

Rich was already moving toward them, his medical instincts kicking in. "Let me see." He gently examined James's hands, then looked up with a reassuring smile. "All good. Just still tender. Janet, you didn't do any damage."

The moment of tension broke, and everyone laughed—the kind of relieved laughter that comes after a scare that turns out to be nothing.

Callum found himself blinking back tears, remembering what Evan used to say about their Christmas parties: "The best gifts are the ones that change you."

Anders was wiping his eyes, not even trying to hide his emotion. When the hugging finally subsided, he looked around the room and said, "Well, shit. How am I supposed to follow that?"

"You don't," Janet said firmly. "That boy just won Christmas."

The rest of the evening passed in a blur of laughter, conversation, and the easy intimacy of people who genuinely cared about each other. James and Anders ended up on the floor by the fireplace, deep in conversation with Tom about his job at the local AIDS clinic. Elena and Sarah had cornered Rich and were grilling him about the hospital's new policies. David and Wynn were debating the merits of various Christmas cookie recipes while Janet listened with the patience of someone who'd mediated far more contentious discussions.

It was Sarah who first noticed the candle beside Evan's angel on the mantle had burned down to a stub, wax pooling around its base.

"Callum," she called softly, "looks like you need a new candle."

Callum glanced over and nodded, heading to the kitchen drawer where he kept spare candles and matches. He rummaged through the contents—batteries, rubber bands, takeout menus—until his fingers found what he was looking for at the back of the drawer. But as he pulled it out, something else came with it.

A small Christmas wreath brooch, covered in green enamel and tiny rhinestones that caught the kitchen light. Evan's brooch. He'd found it at some thrift store years ago and decided it was "perfectly tacky" for their Christmas parties, pinning it to his sweater every year despite Callum's protests that it was meant for an old lady's blouse.

"It sparkles, Cal," Evan would say with that mischievous grin. "It makes me think of my grandmother's Christmas tree. Sometimes you need a little sparkle to cover up the dark parts."

Callum's vision blurred as he stared at the brooch in his palm.

"Everything okay?" Elena appeared beside him, her voice gentle.

He held up the brooch wordlessly, and understanding crossed her face immediately.

"Oh, honey." She took it from his hands, examining the delicate rhinestones. "This is beautiful. Very Evan."

"He wore it every Christmas party," Callum managed. "Said it reminded him of good memories."

Without asking, Elena began pinning the brooch to Callum's sweater. He started to protest—"That was more Evan's thing"—but she shushed him gently.

"Tonight it's your thing too."

James and Anders had noticed the quiet exchange, watching with that careful attention young people pay when they're trying to understand the adults in their lives. Here was Callum—only thirty-six, but carrying the weight of an old widower, moving through his grief with a grace they couldn't fully comprehend.

"Here," Callum said, his voice steadier now as he pulled a fresh candle from the drawer. "Let me replace this."

He moved to the mantle, but as he began to remove the spent candle, something shifted in the room. Conversations quieted.

People turned to watch, as if sensing they were witnessing something sacred.

Callum lit the new candle, its flame casting fresh light on the porcelain angel's serene face. Soft Christmas music played from the stereo, filling the silence that had settled over the room. No one spoke. No one moved.

He'd only meant to replace a candle—something simple, practical. But standing back, Callum looked around the room at all the faces watching him, then back at the angel bathed in fresh candlelight. He managed a small, choked smile and nodded in acknowledgment of what everyone was thinking.

Evan was here. In the flickering flame that watched over their party, in the angel that protected their family, in the love that filled this room he had once filled with his own light.

Callum found himself in the kitchen, loading the dishwasher and trying to process the evening. Through the doorway, he could see James gesturing animatedly as he told some story, completely at ease now, surrounded by people who'd already adopted him as one of their own.

"Evan would have loved him," Sarah said, appearing beside him with an armload of empty plates.

Callum nodded, not trusting his voice.

"He would have loved seeing you happy again too," she added gently.

"I'm not sure I deserve to be happy," Callum said quietly.

"Oh, honey." Sarah set down the plates and turned to face him fully. "You think Evan would want you to spend the rest of your life mourning him? That beautiful man who loved you more than life itself?"

Callum looked through the doorway again, where James was

now helping Anders demonstrate some complicated game involving hand gestures and increasingly silly sound effects.

"He'd want you to love again," Sarah continued. "Maybe not the same way, maybe not romantic love. But this—" she gestured toward the living room "—this is love too. Taking in that boy, giving him a family, letting him heal you as much as you're healing him. That's exactly what Evan would want."

As if sensing he was being discussed, James looked toward the kitchen and caught Callum's eye. He smiled—that slow, genuine smile that had become precious to Callum—and gave a little wave.

Callum waved back, and for the first time since March, the gesture felt like a beginning rather than an ending.

The party wound down gradually, as the best parties do. People lingered over final conversations, reluctant to break the spell of the evening. Rich and Wynn were the last to leave, and Rich pulled Callum aside as they gathered their coats.

"I'm proud of you," he said simply. "And I'm glad you found him. Or he found you. However it worked."

"Thanks for bending the rules," Callum said. "At the hospital, I mean."

"Sometimes the rules need bending." Rich glanced toward the living room, where James and Anders were collecting empty glasses and tidying up without being asked. "Besides, look how it turned out."

After everyone had gone, the three of them worked together to clean up—a comfortable routine that felt like it had been established over years rather than days. James started to wash dishes, but as soon as his hands hit the hot water, he winced and pulled back.

"Okay, new plan," Anders said, gently steering James away from the sink. "You're on supervisor duty. Point and tell us what we're missing."

"I can help—" James started to protest.

"You are helping," Callum said, already taking over the washing. "Management is a very important job."

So James perched on a stool, directing their efforts while Anders dried and Callum washed, and nobody felt the need to fill the comfortable silence with chatter.

"Thank you," James said finally, as they finished the last of the glasses. "For tonight. For all of it."

"Thank *you*," Anders said. "I haven't had that much fun at a party in... well, ever."

"Anders," Callum said, drying his hands on a dish towel, "do you need anything for the guest room? Extra blankets? I think there are fresh towels already up there."

"I'm good, thanks. You've already done too much."

Callum looked at both of them—these two young men who'd wandered into his life and somehow made it worth living again. "Evan always said the best parties were the ones that felt like family," he said. "Tonight felt like family."

James smiled, that soft smile that never failed to catch Callum off guard. "Yeah," he said. "It really did."

As they turned off the lights and headed upstairs together, Callum caught sight of Evan's angel on the mantle, her porcelain face serene in the candlelight that still flickered beside her. For the first time since placing her there, she didn't look like a memorial to the past.

She looked like a blessing on the future.

Twenty

In the space
between heartbeats
lies a lifetime of love,
and in the silence
after all we have left
to speak of.

THE MACHINES HAD BEEN BEEPING STEADILY for hours, their rhythm as familiar to Callum now as his own breathing. He sat in the uncomfortable vinyl chair beside Evan's bed, holding a hand that felt too light, too fragile, like something that might dissolve if he loosened his grip.

The room was dim, lit only by the soft glow of monitors and the hallway light seeping under the door. Visiting hours had ended long ago, but the nurses had stopped trying to make him leave. Rich had seen to that, bending rules that seemed meaningless in the face of what was happening here.

Evan's breathing was shallow, labored, his mouth hanging open as if he couldn't draw enough air no matter how hard he tried. His jaw seemed too tired to close, muscles too weak for even that small effort. The man Callum had fallen in love with—small but fierce, always in motion—now looked impossibly fragile against the white hospital sheets, his once-bright eyes sunken in a face that had grown gaunt over these final weeks.

Callum tried to look beyond the dark splotches that had spread across Evan's cheek against his pale, waxy skin. All he could see was the beauty Evan had always possessed—that flawless complexion and unfair youth that required no effort and turned heads wherever they went. It seemed impossibly cruel that this disease could so deliberately steal away the very thing that had first caught Callum's attention in that theatre classroom seventeen years ago.

His eyes were closed, had been for most of the day, but occasionally they would flutter open, searching until they found Callum's face.

"Still here," Callum would whisper, and Evan would manage the ghost of a smile.

They were past tears now. Past desperate bargaining with a God that neither of them had ever fully believed in. Past the rage at the unfairness of thirty-five being too young, too soon, too fucking cruel. Now there was only this: the weight of Evan's hand in his, the sound of labored breathing, and the terrible knowledge that time was running out in ways that couldn't be measured by clocks.

Evan's eyes opened again, focusing with effort on Callum's face.

"Hey," Callum whispered, leaning closer.

Evan's lips moved, and Callum had to strain to hear the words. "Remember... Theatre... class?"

A smile tugged at the corner of Callum's mouth despite

everything. "You mean when you sat next to me and asked if you were late?"

"Not... accident," Evan breathed, and there was the faintest hint of his old mischief in his eyes. "Saw you... wanted to... know you."

It had been seventeen years ago, in that theatre classroom with "My Sharona" playing on the radio. Callum had been this nervous farm boy, afraid to take up space, when Evan had swept in late and chosen the seat right next to him.

"You're cute," Evan had whispered during that first class. "Want to work with me?" And somehow, in that moment, everything had changed.

That had been Evan—fearless and direct, turning chance encounters into destiny, finding ways to claim the things and people he wanted. They'd spent seventeen years together after that first bold move, Evan teaching him what it meant to be loved without reservation.

"You didn't pretend it was an accident," Callum said now, his thumb tracing gentle circles on Evan's wrist. "You told me later. You saw me sitting there and thought I looked lonely. Chose to sit next to me on purpose."

"Did." Evan's voice was barely audible. "Wanted... to know... you."

"Best decision you ever made."

Evan's grip tightened slightly, summoning strength from somewhere. "Love you... Cal... So... much."

"I love you too." The words came out steady, though Callum's chest felt like it was caving in. "I love you so much."

"Take care... of... yourself... Promise... me."

Callum's throat closed. He couldn't promise that, couldn't promise anything beyond this moment. But Evan was looking at him with those eyes that had always seen straight through to his heart, waiting for an answer that mattered more than any vow they'd ever exchanged.

"I promise," he whispered, though he had no idea how he would keep it.

Evan's eyes drifted closed, his breathing growing more shallow. The monitors continued their steady beeping, marking time in a way that felt both eternal and impossibly brief.

"The angel," Evan whispered suddenly, his eyes still closed. "Mantle... She'll... watch... over... you."

"Evan—"

"Promise... me."

"I promise."

A small smile crossed Evan's lips. "Good."

His breathing grew quieter, more spaced apart, his mouth still hanging open in that desperate search for air. Callum held his hand tighter, as if his own life force could somehow bridge the gap that was widening between them.

"I'm here," he whispered. "I'm right here."

Evan's lips moved one last time, shaping words too quiet for sound. But Callum read them anyway: *I know.*

The machines continued their electronic symphony for a few more minutes—steady beeps that had become the soundtrack of their vigil. Evan's breathing grew fainter, more irregular, until suddenly his chest rose sharply in one final, desperate gasp for air.

Then he relaxed completely, his face peaceful for the first time in weeks, and the rhythm changed.

A long, steady tone filled the room.

Callum sat in the sudden silence, still holding Evan's hand, still feeling the warmth that hadn't yet faded. He didn't call for nurses. He didn't cry. He didn't move.

He held Evan's hand.

Twenty-One

In the quiet before dawn
two hearts find their way,
and learn that sometimes
healing begins with
what we cannot say.

JAMES HAD BEEN awake for over an hour, staring at the ceiling in what had become his room—though he still couldn't quite believe that phrase applied to him. *His* room. The concept felt foreign, like trying on clothes that were the right size but still didn't quite fit.

He'd tried to fall back asleep, but his mind was restless, cycling through the events of the previous evening. The party, the warmth of all those people, the way they'd embraced him like he'd always belonged there. It felt like something out of a dream, the kind of belonging he'd imagined but never actually experienced.

But lying there in the dark, another realization had crept in with startling clarity: he could have died. Really died. Not in some abstract, dramatic way, but actually frozen to death in an alley, alone and forgotten. The thought hit him with a force it hadn't carried before, when he'd been focused on recovery and trying to figure out where he fit in Callum's world.

He'd been nineteen years old and nearly died because he had nowhere to go.

The weight of it pressed against his chest until he couldn't lie still any longer. Pulling on the soft sweatshirt Callum had given him—Evan's sweatshirt, though James tried not to think about that too much—he padded downstairs in his bare feet, drawn by an impulse he couldn't name.

The parlor was dark except for the streetlight filtering through the front windows, casting long shadows across the furniture. James moved quietly to the mantle where Evan's angel stood, her porcelain face serene in the dim light. The candle beside her had burned down to a stub, but he found matches in the drawer beneath and lit a fresh one, the small flame immediately warming the angel's features.

Then he plugged in the Christmas tree lights, and the room transformed. Hundreds of tiny bulbs reflected off the ornaments, casting dancing patterns on the walls and ceiling. It was magical in the way Christmas mornings were supposed to be when you were a kid waiting for Santa, except James had never really had mornings like that. His family had done Christmas, but it had always felt obligatory, perfunctory. This felt different. This felt like wonder.

He settled onto the sofa, pulling his feet up and wrapping his arms around his knees, just staring. At the tree, at the angel, at this room that somehow felt more like home than anywhere he'd ever lived.

"Is it okay if I sit?"

The whispered voice startled him, and he looked up to find Anders standing in the doorway, his hair messed from sleep, wearing a t-shirt and boxers. He looked young and uncertain, like he was afraid he might be intruding.

"Of course," James whispered back, patting the space beside him on the sofa.

Anders settled next to him, careful not to sit too close, and for a while they just existed in the quiet together. The tree lights blinked in their slow rhythm, the candle flickered beside the angel, and outside, the world was still and dark.

"Couldn't sleep either?" Anders asked eventually.

"Too much in my head, I guess," James said. "Last night was... a lot."

"Good lot or overwhelming lot?"

James considered this. "Both, maybe. Good, definitely. But also..." He struggled for the words. "I keep thinking about how I almost didn't make it to see any of this. Like, really almost didn't make it."

Anders was quiet for a moment. "When Callum called to invite me to the party, he told me what happened. About you nearly freezing in that alley... Jesus, James. We could have lost you before we even really found you."

There was something in Anders's voice, a genuine fear and protectiveness, that made James's chest tight. When was the last time someone had worried about losing him?

"What about you?" James asked. "Why are you awake?"

Anders smiled ruefully. "Thinking about how different everything is. A week ago I was just this guy living with Marcus and Trevor, working at the gallery, going through the motions. Now I'm here, in this house, with you and Callum, and it's like..." He paused. "It's like my whole life just shifted, and I don't know what comes next."

"Scary?"

"Terrifying," Anders admitted. "But also exciting. Like maybe there are good things waiting that I hadn't even thought to hope for."

They fell quiet again, both lost in their own thoughts. James found himself studying Anders's profile in the soft light—the gentle curve of his jaw, the way his eyelashes cast shadows on his cheeks, the small scar on his forehead that James had never noticed before.

"Janet was funny last night," James said eventually. "The way she just announced that David's cookies were terrible."

Anders laughed softly. "Right to his face. I love that about her. No filter, but you know she means well."

"And Rich's partner—Wynn. He seemed really kind."

"Wynn's great. He works with kids who've been in the system. Has this way of making everyone feel safe." Anders glanced at James. "I think that's why Rich wanted you to meet him. Figured you'd understand each other."

James nodded, thinking about the easy way Wynn had talked to him, like James was worth listening to. "Elena told me about her garden. Wants to teach me about growing vegetables in the spring."

"That sounds nice. You'd be good at that."

"How do you know?"

Anders turned to face him more fully. "Because you're careful with things. Gentle. I watched you with those ornaments the other night, how you handled them like they mattered."

The observation touched something deep in James's chest. "I've never had anything that was worth being careful with before."

"Now you do."

Their eyes met in the tree lights, and James felt something shift between them—not dramatic, just a quiet recognition, like puzzle pieces settling into place.

"Anders," James said carefully, "what happened to Evan? Callum doesn't really talk about it, and I don't want to pry, but..."

Anders was quiet for a long moment. "I was at the funeral," he said finally. "I didn't know him well, but the whole community came out. He was... he was really loved."

"But what did he die of?"

"AIDS," Anders said gently. "I'm pretty sure, anyway. There were... you could tell, toward the end."

James felt his stomach drop. "Does that mean Callum...?"

"I don't know. I hope not. But that's probably part of why losing Evan was so devastating. It wasn't just losing his partner, it was losing his whole future, and maybe wondering about his own." Anders's voice was barely a whisper. "I can't imagine that kind of fear."

They sat with that weight for a while, both thinking about Callum upstairs, about the man who had taken James in without hesitation despite carrying his own overwhelming grief.

"He saved my life," James said eventually.

"You saved his too," Anders replied. "You just don't realize it yet."

James looked at him questioningly.

"Last night, watching him with you, with all of us—that was the first time I've seen him really present since the funeral. Like he remembered how to be happy."

"I don't feel like I'm doing anything special."

"That's exactly what makes it special." Anders shifted slightly closer on the sofa. "You're just being yourself, James. And yourself is worth saving."

The sincerity in his voice made James's eyes sting. "I'm not used to people talking to me like that."

"Like what?"

"Like I matter."

Anders reached out then, slowly, giving James time to pull away if he wanted to. When James didn't move, Anders's fingers brushed against his, then carefully intertwined with them. James's hands were still tender from the frostbite, so Anders was extraordinarily gentle, holding on just firmly enough to make the connection real.

"You matter to me," Anders said simply.

James looked down at their joined hands, marveling at how right it felt. "This is probably crazy, isn't it? Everything that's happened, how fast it's all changed?"

"Probably," Anders agreed. "Does that bother you?"

James considered this. "It should. I mean, a week ago I didn't even know if I'd survive the winter, and now I'm sitting in this beautiful house holding hands with someone who..." He trailed off, blushing.

"Someone who what?"

"Someone I can't stop thinking about," James admitted quietly.

Anders's smile was soft and wondering. "Good. Because I've been thinking about you too. Ever since Halloween, if I'm being honest."

"Really?"

"Really. But James..." Anders's expression grew more serious. "I don't want to rush anything. You've been through so much, and you're still healing, and I don't want to be another thing that complicates your life."

"You're not complicating anything," James said quickly. "You're the first thing that's felt simple in months."

They looked at each other in the flickering candlelight, both young men who'd been hurt by the people who were supposed to love them, now finding something gentle and hopeful in each other.

"How old are you?" James asked suddenly.

"Twenty-five. Is that weird? The age thing?"

James shook his head. "I was just thinking about how different we are. Like, you've got your life figured out, and I'm still..."

"Figuring it out?"

"I don't even know where to start figuring it out."

Anders squeezed his hand gently. "That's okay. You don't have to have it all figured out. I sure as hell don't, and I'm six years older than you."

"What do you want?" James asked. "I mean, for the future?"

Anders was quiet for a moment, thinking. "A week ago, I would have said I wanted to get back on my feet, maybe find my own place eventually, stop being Marcus and Trevor's charity case." He glanced around the room. "But now? I want to be part of this. Whatever this is. I want to help Callum figure out how to be happy again. I want to watch you discover who you are when you're not just trying to survive." He looked directly at James. "And I want to see where this goes, between us, if you want that too."

"I do," James said without hesitation. "Want that, I mean. I'm just scared I don't know how to do any of it. The relationship thing, the family thing, even just living in a real house with people who actually want me here."

"We'll figure it out together," Anders said. "All of us. Callum's learning too, you know. How to be someone's family when he's spent nine months thinking his family was over."

Through the front windows, the sky was beginning to lighten—not quite sunrise, but that deep blue that comes just before. The angel seemed to glow brighter in her candlelight, watching over them with her serene smile.

"I wish I had presents," James said suddenly. "For you, for Callum. It's Christmas morning and I don't have anything to give."

"You've already given me more than you know," Anders said softly.

"Like what?"

"Hope. For the first time since my family threw me out, I actually believe good things can happen. That people can choose to love each other, even when they're not supposed to." Anders lifted their joined hands and pressed a soft kiss to James's knuckles, careful of his healing skin. "That's worth more than any present."

James felt tears prick his eyes. "I've never had anyone say things like that to me."

"You will now," Anders promised. "From me, from Callum, from all of us. You're part of the family now, James. This crazy family of ours.

Outside, the first hints of gold appeared on the horizon, and the Christmas tree lights seemed to pulse brighter in response. James leaned against Anders's shoulder, solid and warm."

Merry Christmas, Anders," he whispered.

"Merry Christmas, James."

The angel kept her vigil as the sun rose over their little family.

Twenty-Two

The gifts that matter most
are never found beneath a tree,
but in the hearts that open wide
to let love's light shine free.

WHEN CALLUM CAME DOWNSTAIRS AROUND eight, he found Anders and James in the kitchen, both looking slightly sheepish as they attempted to make breakfast. The counter was dusted with flour, there were eggshells in the bowl, and something was definitely burning on the stove.

"We were trying to surprise you," James said, turning from the stove with a spatula in his bandaged hand. "But I think we're failing."

"Spectacularly," Anders added, turning off the burner under what had been pancakes but now resembled charcoal discs. "Turns out neither of us can actually cook."

Callum laughed, the first genuine laugh he'd had on

Christmas morning in years. "The thought counts. But maybe we should salvage what we can and call it good?"

They managed to rescue some eggs and a few pancakes, and settled around the kitchen table with coffee that was surprisingly good. Outside, snow had begun falling again, large flakes drifting past the window in the grey morning light.

"I have something for you both," Callum said when they'd finished eating. "Nothing fancy, but... well, it's Christmas."

James looked immediately uncomfortable. "Callum, I told you, I don't have anything to give you. I wanted to, but—"

"James." Callum's voice was gentle but firm. "You've already given me more than you know. Both of you have."

He disappeared upstairs and returned with several wrapped packages—clearly done hastily, with uneven edges and too much tape, but wrapped with obvious care.

"Anders first," he said, setting a rectangular package in front of him.

Anders unwrapped it carefully, his eyes widening as he revealed a set of art supplies—tubes of acrylic paint in primary colors, a set of colored pencils, and a pad of drawing paper. But it was what was clipped to the front of the pad that made his breath catch.

A drawing—crude but purposeful—showed three stick figures holding hands. One tall, one medium, one smaller. They were rendered in colored pencil with the unsteady hand of someone who hadn't drawn since elementary school, but every line was deliberate. Above them, Callum had written in careful block letters: "FAMILY."

"I know I'm not much of an artist," Callum said, suddenly self-conscious. "But I wanted you to know... what this means. What you both mean. The three of us, we're..." He gestured helplessly at the drawing. "That's supposed to be us. Family."

Anders stared at the drawing, his eyes bright with unshed tears. "Callum, this is... God, this is perfect."

"The supplies aren't much, but I remembered you mentioning you used to draw, before everything happened. Thought maybe you'd like to again."

"I'd forgotten," Anders said quietly, running his fingers over the pencils. "How much I missed it." He looked up at Callum. "Thank you. Really."

Callum turned to James, who was watching the exchange with something like wonder. "Your turn."

There were several packages for James, and he opened them with the careful attention of someone who'd rarely received gifts. Jeans that actually fit, a heavy sweater, warm socks, a winter hat. Each item was practical but chosen with obvious thought.

"How did you know my size?" James asked, holding up the jeans.

"Lucky guessing. Though I may have peeked at the clothes you were wearing when you came to the hospital."

The next package contained a Walkman—one of the newer portable CD players—along with a small stack of CDs. James read the titles aloud: "Alanis Morissette's *Jagged Little Pill*, Bush's *Sixteen Stone*, Oasis's *What's the Story Morning Glory*..." He looked up, overwhelmed. "Callum, this is too much."

"I didn't know what kind of music you liked," Callum admitted. "So I asked the guy at the record store what was popular with people your age. He seemed confident about those choices."

"They're perfect," James said, though his voice was thick with emotion. "I can't believe you did all this."

"There's one more," Callum said quietly, sliding a final package across the table.

This one was smaller, wrapped in simple brown paper. When James unwrapped it, he revealed a leather-bound journal, the kind with unlined pages and a ribbon bookmark. The leather was soft and worn, obviously not new.

"It was Evan's," Callum said. "He bought it years ago but never wrote in it. Always said he was waiting for something important enough to fill it." He paused. "I think he would have wanted you to have it."

James opened the cover and froze. Inside, tucked against the first page, was an envelope with his name written in Callum's careful handwriting. His hands trembled slightly as he pulled it out.

"Go ahead," Callum said softly. "Read it."

James glanced at Anders, who nodded encouragingly, then carefully opened the envelope. Inside was a folded letter—several pages written in the same neat script—and something else that caught the light. A key.

As James unfolded the letter and began to read, his expression shifted from curiosity to disbelief to overwhelming emotion. Anders watched, concerned, as tears began streaming down James's face. The silence in the kitchen stretched, broken only by the soft sound of James's breathing and the tick of the wall clock.

When he finished reading, James set the letter down with shaking hands and looked at Callum with an expression of such raw gratitude and love that Anders felt like he was intruding on something sacred.

Without a word, James stood and crossed to Callum, practically falling into his arms. His shoulders shook with silent sobs as Callum held him, one hand stroking his hair, murmuring quiet reassurances.

"It's okay," Callum whispered. "It's all okay."

Anders half-rose from his chair, worried, but Callum caught his eye over James's head and gave him a small shake of his head —not dismissive, but reassuring. *It's okay. This is what he needed.*

After several minutes, James pulled back, wiping his eyes

with the back of his hand. "I'm sorry," he said, his voice hoarse. "I just... I can't..."

"You don't need to apologize," Callum said firmly. "And you don't need to say anything. That was between us."

James nodded, still crying but smiling now. He picked up the key from where it had fallen on the table, holding it like it was made of precious metal.

"What's the key for?" Anders asked gently.

Callum and James exchanged a look—private, meaningful.

"Home," James said simply, and closed his fingers around the key.

Anders felt something shift in his chest, a mixture of joy for James and a strange wistfulness he couldn't name. He was happy, genuinely happy for this moment, for what it meant to James. But part of him wondered where he fit in this new configuration, what his place would be in this family that was forming around him.

As if sensing his thoughts, Callum reached across the table and squeezed Anders's hand. "All of us," he said quietly. "The drawing wasn't just for show, Anders. You're part of this too."

Anders nodded, not trusting his voice. Outside, the snow continued to fall, and inside, something precious and fragile and perfect was taking shape among the three of them. It didn't look like any family Anders had ever known, but it felt more real than anything he'd ever experienced.

"Merry Christmas," James said, his voice still shaky but filled with something that might have been hope.

"Merry Christmas," Callum and Anders replied in unison.

It truly was.

Twenty-Three

In the quiet spaces
between words
hearts find their truest voice,
and souls learn
that being heard
is sometimes
healing's greatest choice.

THE AFTERNOON HAD PASSED in the kind of lazy contentment that made perfect Christmas days—the three of them sprawled around the dining room table with board games spread between them, arguing over Scrabble rules and laughing until their sides hurt. James had discovered Evan's game collection in what Callum called "Evan's Mess"—though Evan had always insisted it be called "The Gift Wrapping Room"—and they'd worked their way through Monopoly, Yahtzee, and now this heated Scrabble debate.

179

"'Razzmatazz' is absolutely a word," Callum insisted, arranging his tiles with theatrical precision. "It means flashy showmanship. Evan used it all the time."

"Just because Evan said it doesn't make it a real word!" James protested, though he was grinning. "That's not how dictionaries work!"

"I'm with James on this one," Anders said, trying to look serious despite the smile tugging at his lips. "Seven letters, triple word score, and it's probably made up."

"Traitor!" Callum exclaimed with mock outrage. "Siding with your boyfriend against me!"

The word hung in the air for a moment—*boyfriend*—and James felt his cheeks warm as he glanced at Anders. Are we? The question was written clearly on his face, and Anders felt his own flush rise in response.

"Well," Callum continued, oblivious to the exchange, "I'm playing it anyway. House rules." He placed the tiles with a flourish just as the winter light began fading outside the dining room windows.

"I should probably start thinking about dinner," Callum said, stretching. "Given this morning's culinary disaster."

They cleaned up the games together, Callum and Anders carrying the boxes back to Evan's room while James sorted the Scrabble tiles. In the small, cluttered space that still smelled faintly of Evan's cologne, Anders couldn't contain his curiosity any longer.

"Are we?" he asked quietly as they stacked game boxes on the shelf. "Like... boyfriends?"

Anders looked uncertain, almost shy. "I mean, we haven't even kissed yet."

"Well," James said softly, moving closer, "that can be rectified."

It was gentle, tentative—more question than statement.

Anders's hand came up to cup James's face, thumb brushing over his cheekbone, and when their lips met it was soft and warm and perfect. James felt something settle in his chest, like a piece of himself he hadn't known was missing finally clicking into place.

"Dinner!" Callum's voice echoed from downstairs, and they broke apart, both breathless and grinning.

"To be continued?" Anders whispered.

"Definitely," James whispered back.

After dinner—which Callum had managed without burning anything—they'd settled in the parlor. Callum tended to the candle beside Evan's angel, something Anders noticed he'd been more attentive to since Christmas Eve. The flame cast dancing shadows on the porcelain face, and for a moment Callum just stood there, lost in some private conversation.

"I'm going to make cookies," James announced from his spot on the sofa. "Pillsbury, but still. And hot chocolate for everyone."

"You don't have to—" Callum started.

"I want to," James said firmly. "Let me do something nice for you guys for once."

As James disappeared into the kitchen, the parlor grew quiet except for the soft crackling of logs in the fireplace. Anders studied Callum's profile in the flickering light, this man who had somehow become central to both their lives in such a short time.

"He seems happier," Anders said quietly.

Callum settled into his armchair, cradling his coffee mug. "He does. You both do."

"It's because of you. What you've done for him... for both of us."

"I think it's more complicated than that," Callum said. "But Anders, I wanted to talk to you. About you, specifically. We've spent so much time focused on James's situation, but you've got your own journey."

Anders felt something shift uncomfortably in his chest. "I'm fine. Really."

"Are you?" Callum's voice was gentle but probing. "Because I know what it's like to carry things alone, and I suspect you've been doing that for a while now."

Anders was quiet for a long moment, staring into the fire. When he finally spoke, his voice was barely above a whisper. "Sometimes I feel like I'm still that kid getting beaten up in Chicago, you know? Like no matter how far I've come, how much Marcus and Trevor have helped me, I'm still just... taking up space that belongs to someone else."

"What do you mean?"

"I mean living at their house, eating their food, using their utilities. They keep saying I'm not a burden, but..." Anders's hands clenched in his lap. "I'm twenty-five years old, Callum. I should have my own place by now. I should be self-sufficient."

"Says who?"

The question caught Anders off guard. "What?"

"Who decided that twenty-five means you should have everything figured out? That needing help makes you less worthy of it?"

"I... everyone knows that. You're supposed to be independent by—"

"Anders." Callum leaned forward, his voice firm but kind. "Listen to me. Marcus and Trevor aren't keeping you around out of pity. They've told you that, haven't they?"

"Yeah, but—"

"But nothing. You think they'd lie to you? You think they'd keep someone in their home for almost a year if they didn't genuinely want you there?"

Anders felt tears prick his eyes. "It's hard to believe sometimes."

"I understand that. When you've been thrown away by the people who were supposed to love you unconditionally, it becomes hard to trust that anyone else's love is real." Callum set down his mug and looked directly at Anders. "But their love is real. And so is mine. And so is James's."

The tears spilled over then, and Anders wiped them away quickly. "I'm sorry, I don't know why I'm—"

"Don't apologize. You have nothing to apologize for."

They sat in comfortable silence while Anders collected himself, the only sounds the fire crackling and the faint noise of James moving around in the kitchen.

"I want to tell you something," Callum continued. "You're welcome here, Anders. In this house, I mean. James's and my house. You're welcome here any time, for any reason."

"That's very kind, but—"

"I'm not done." Callum smiled gently. "However, I think you should stay at Brooke Street for now."

Anders looked confused. "I don't understand."

"What I mean is, don't feel like you need to find your own place to prove something. Marcus and Trevor are right—you belong there. But also don't feel like you need to move in here just because James is here." Callum paused, choosing his words carefully. "You two are just starting to figure out what this is between you. Having some space, some breathing room, might be good for both of you. It's not far between here and Brooke Street. You can see each other whenever you want, but you each have your own spaces to retreat to when you need them."

"That is..." He nodded, not sure how to finish his sentence.

"Evan and I were practically living together after three weeks of dating," Callum said with a rueful smile. "Crammed into those tiny dorm beds, mostly mine because my roommate was cool with it. We were lucky it worked out, but looking back, we probably should have taken our time. There's no rush, Anders. Let this develop naturally."

Anders nodded, feeling some tension he hadn't even realized he'd been carrying start to ease. "Thank you. For listening. For... seeing me, I guess."

"Of course I see you. You're family now." Callum reached into his pocket and pulled out a small object, pressing it into Anders's palm. A house key. "You might not live here, but there's no reason you shouldn't have this. Come and go as you and James want. Invite him to your place sometimes. Enjoy discovering each other."

Anders stared at the key, overwhelmed. "Callum, I can't—"

"You can and you will. That key represents something important, Anders. It means you belong somewhere. It means you have people who want you around, who trust you, who consider you family." Callum's voice was warm but firm. "Don't you dare feel guilty about accepting it."

Anders closed his fingers around the key, feeling its weight. "How do you do it?"

"Do what?"

"Make people feel like they matter. Like they're worth something."

Callum was quiet for a moment. "I don't think I do anything special. I think I just remember what it felt like when Evan did it for me, and I try to pass that forward."

"He must have been amazing."

"He was. And he would have loved both of you. Probably would have adopted you both within five minutes of meeting you." Callum smiled softly. "He had a gift for seeing people who needed family and making them part of his world."

The sound of James's footsteps interrupted the moment, and

Anders quickly wiped his eyes, tucking the key safely into his pocket.

"I'll tell him later," Anders said quietly. "About the key, the conversation. Is that okay?"

"Of course. Take your time."

James appeared in the doorway carrying a tray of cookies and three mugs of hot chocolate, his face bright with the simple pleasure of doing something nice for the people he cared about.

"Perfect timing," Callum said, making room on the coffee table. "We were just talking about how lucky we are."

"Lucky how?" James asked, settling onto the sofa next to Anders.

Anders caught Callum's eye and smiled. "Lucky to have found each other," he said simply.

James leaned against Anders's shoulder, and Callum watched them with something that might have been contentment. Outside, snow continued to fall, and inside, their family grew stronger with each quiet moment shared.

Twenty-Four

*Some words are written
not with ink but with the courage of a heart
that chooses love over endings,
and hope over falling apart.*

"I THINK I'm going to head up to bed," Callum said, stretching as he rose from his armchair. "It's been a perfect day, but I'm exhausted."

James and Anders were settled on the sofa together, the remnants of their hot chocolate and cookies on the coffee table between them. The parlor glowed with warmth—the Christmas tree lights twinkling against the glass ornaments, the fire crackling softly in the fireplace, and outside the front windows, snow continued to fall under the amber glow of the streetlamp.

"Goodnight, Callum," James said softly. "And thank you. For everything today."

"Thank you both," Callum replied. "Sweet dreams."

As his footsteps faded up the stairs, the parlor settled into peaceful quiet. James shifted closer to Anders on the sofa, and without thinking, Anders wrapped his arm around him, pulling him against his side. James nestled into the embrace with a contented sigh, his head resting on Anders's shoulder.

This, Anders thought, was the best Christmas present he could have imagined. Not the art supplies or even Callum's touching drawing, but this—James warm and trusting in his arms, the two of them safe and wanted in this beautiful room that was beginning to feel like home.

They sat in comfortable silence, watching the flames dance in the fireplace, both lost in their own thoughts about how dramatically their lives had changed in just a few days.

"James?" Anders said finally, his voice barely above a whisper.

"Mmm?"

Anders hesitated, then curiosity got the better of him. "What did that letter say?" He caught himself immediately, shaking his head. "Sorry, nevermind. That was for you. I'm being nosy."

James lifted his head from Anders's shoulder and sat up, his expression unreadable. Without a word, he stood and headed toward the stairs, leaving Anders alone on the sofa, immediately regretting his question.

Shit, Anders thought. Had he pushed too hard? Callum had just told him to take things slow, to let their relationship develop naturally. James was still vulnerable, still healing. Maybe sharing something that personal was too much to ask.

Anders sat alone, staring at the candle flickering beside Evan's angel on the mantle. The flame cast dancing shadows across her serene face, and he could understand why Evan had treasured her so much. There was something soothing about her presence, like she was indeed watching over them.

He was so absorbed in studying the angel that he didn't notice James had returned until he heard a soft clearing of the throat. James stood beside the sofa, holding several folded sheets of paper.

"I... I don't have to read it," Anders said quickly. "I'm sorry. It's personal between you and—"

"I want you to," James interrupted, settling back down beside him.

"Really?"

James nodded, studying Anders's face with those earnest eyes. "I want you to understand. What this means. What he's given me."

With trembling hands, Anders unfolded the letter. The paper was cream-colored, quality stationery, and every word was written in Callum's careful penmanship—the kind of hand-writing that took time and deliberate effort, as if he'd known how important these words would be.

Anders began to read:

My Dear James,

I am writing this letter on Christmas Eve, after watching you with our friends tonight, after seeing you discover what it means to belong some-where. I wanted to put into words what I haven't been able to say aloud—what you mean to me, and what I hope I can mean to you.

I need to tell you something about the night we met. Before I came into that restaurant, before I saw you standing behind that counter, I had made a decision. I couldn't bear the loneliness anymore, James. The ghost of Evan in every corner of this house, in every photograph, in every memory that used to bring joy but had become unbearable weight. I had been saving up one small shred of hope—just enough to get me through one final task. And then I was going to let go.

But I saw you, James. Not just what you wore or what you said, but something deeper. I saw your profound despair, your hopelessness, and I recognized it because I was drowning in the same dark water. In that moment, I realized that the sliver of hope I had been saving for myself was better suited as a gift for someone else. Someone who needed it more than I did.

And that someone was you.

I cannot control what happened in your life before we met, and I am terribly sorry to know that someone as wonderful as the man I witness before me today was cast aside by people who should have treasured you. But I recognize the wonder in you, James. I see your talent, your capacity for joy that bubbles just beneath the surface, your drive and tenacity to live if you could only hang on to hope. And that is where I can help.

A home, yes—here is the key, and it is yours for as long as you want it. But more than that,

I can offer you something at my own expense: that sliver of hope that Evan left for me to hold onto. The promise he made me just before he died—to take care of myself—I give that promise to you now. What you do with it, I cannot know. But as long as I have the ability, I will always be here with and around you, helping you look toward the opportunities ahead while I shield you from the pain of the road behind. We'll take only what is valuable from your past and leave the rest.

James, you are loved. By me, by Anders, by all the people who welcomed you into their hearts last night, and by many more who will come into your life. But I freely offer you this Christmas something of which I can never give away again: my love, my support, my protection, and my faith in who you are becoming. Never question that I will be here for you, just as I trust you will be there for someone in need someday, passing forward what you have received.

You saved my life by letting me save yours. The gift you hoped to give me—your trust, your presence in my home—pales in comparison to what you gave me without realizing it: a reason to keep living, a purpose beyond my grief, and the chance to love again in a way I thought had died with Evan.

191

Welcome home, son.

With all my love,
Callum

P.S. Evan would have adored you. He had a gift for seeing people who needed family and making them part of his world instantly. I'm certain he's watching over us all, probably delighted that his angel is keeping watch over such a beautiful new family.

Anders's hands shook as he finished reading. Tears rolled down his cheeks, and he carefully folded the letter, handing it back to James with the reverence it deserved.

"God, James," he whispered, his voice thick with emotion. "You're so lucky to have found him."

"*We're* so lucky," James corrected gently, settling back against Anders's side.

Anders wrapped his arms around James again, this time with a deeper understanding of what they'd all found in each other. They gazed into the fire, then turned their attention back to the angel on the mantle, her candle still flickering steadily.

Anders began gently playing with James's hair, running his fingers through the soft strands as James shifted to lay his head in his lap. Slowly, James's eyes drifted closed, his breathing becoming deep and even.

In the warm glow of the Christmas tree and the dancing fire-light, with snow falling softly outside and Evan's angel keeping watch, Anders felt a peace he'd never known was possible. They were all broken in their own ways—Callum with his grief, James with his abandonment, Anders with his own family's betrayal. But somehow, together, they were becoming whole.

As James slept peacefully, Anders whispered a quiet thank you to the angel, to Evan's memory, and to whatever force had brought them all together on that stormy December night. They were family now—chosen, fought for, and cherished. And that was worth more than any gift under any Christmas tree.

Twenty-Five

Love never truly leaves us—
it transforms
it transcends,
and in the hearts that remain
its light forever extends.

"OH MY GOD, Cal, look at this place!" Evan's voice echoed through the empty rooms as he practically bounced from space to space, his footsteps loud on the hardwood floors that hadn't seen care in decades.

Callum followed more cautiously, clipboard in hand, making mental notes about structural issues and renovation costs. The house on St. James Court was a Victorian dream wrapped in a 1970s nightmare—avocado green kitchen appliances, shag carpeting so matted it looked like it could be sheared, and wallpaper that belonged in a psychedelic fever dream.

"None of these houses ever come up for sale," their realtor

had told them breathlessly. "The owner just passed, and the adult children live out of state. For them, it's just a real estate transaction, but for the right buyers..." She'd trailed off meaningfully.

Evan could see past all of it. As he walked through each room, his hands gestured wildly, painting pictures in the air. "We'll strip all this wallpaper, restore the original crown molding, and these floors—Cal, these floors will be gorgeous once we refinish them. And the kitchen! We'll gut the whole thing, put in something period-appropriate but functional."

Callum watched his partner with amused affection, trying to balance Evan's enthusiasm with practical concerns. "Evan, the restoration alone will cost a fortune. And look at this chimney work..."

But Evan had moved on to the parlor, standing transfixed in the doorway. "Oh, Cal," he whispered, and something in his voice made Callum stop calculating and really look.

The room was magnificent underneath its dated disguise. High ceilings, built-in bookcases, a massive fireplace with an ornate mantelpiece that someone had painted over but couldn't hide the beautiful carved details underneath. And the windows —huge picture windows that would flood the room with light.

Evan walked slowly to the mantelpiece, running his hands over the painted surface. "This needs complete restoration," he said softly. "Paint stripping, patching, probably chimney work too." He turned toward the windows. "But Cal, can you picture it? We could have a huge Christmas tree right here, and..." He paused, his eyes shining. "And here's the perfect spot for Grandma's angel!"

Callum had never seen Evan look so certain about anything. In that moment, standing in a room that needed everything but somehow felt like home, Callum knew they'd found their place.

"Who builds houses like this anymore, Cal?" Evan asked, spinning around to face him. "It's meant to be ours."

Callum stood barefoot at the mantelpiece in his flannel pajamas, but something was wrong. The Christmas tree glowed softly beside him, the fire had burned down to embers, and the house was perfectly quiet. He must have come downstairs during the night, though he couldn't remember doing so.

But the angel—Evan's most prized possession—wasn't there.

He rubbed his eyes, certain he was still half-asleep. Where was she? James and Anders wouldn't have moved her, would they? No, they understood how important she was.

"Cal?"

He spun around at the sound of his name, spoken in a voice he knew better than his own.

Because he had heard a ghost.

Evan stood—or seemed to stand—in the middle of the parlor, his image flowing in and out of focus like heat waves rising from summer pavement. But it was unmistakably him: small and fierce and radiant with that energy that had always made him seem larger than life.

Callum took a step forward, not caring if he should be frightened. He wanted Evan—hallucination or not, dream or vision, he didn't care.

But his feet felt rooted to the floor, no matter how hard he tried to move.

"Cal? Why are you struggling?"

"I can't move," Callum said, his voice breaking.

"No, Cal," Evan's image shimmered closer. "That's not what I meant. Why are you struggling?"

"I... I don't know what you're asking me, Evan." All his carefully maintained composure crumbled. He'd thought he was better, thought he'd processed his grief, thought everyone was right when they said James had helped him get over Evan. But here, faced with this impossible presence, he fell apart completely.

"Evan, I can't do this. You left me! You left and I..." The words poured out in a torrent of pain he'd kept buried for months.

Evan's luminous form moved closer, and Callum felt something like warmth brush against his cheek, drying his tears. "Cal, you're such a mess! I go away for one second and you fall to pieces. It's just like the old days."

Despite everything, Callum laughed through his tears. That was his Evan—sassy and irreverent even as a ghost.

He knew this was a dream.

"I'm here, Cal."

He knew he'd wake up in his bed soon.

"I'm not going away, Cal."

He knew the stress of the past week was playing tricks on his mind.

"Cal, look at me."

But he still wanted to pretend...

"Look at me!"

The room suddenly blazed with light—warm yellows and whites streaked with blue and purple, surrounding Callum like the aurora borealis. And there stood Evan again, not fully formed but unmistakable: the tiny man with the larger-than-life spirit.

Callum almost laughed at his own thought. Larger-than-life spirit.

"And that's what I am, babe."

The endearment broke something open in Callum's chest. 'Babe'—the last word Evan had spoken to him in that hospital room.

"No, no, no," Callum squeezed his eyes shut. "This is all a dream. This is cruel. I can't see you and lose you again. I can't go through your funeral again."

"Cal... have you kept your promise?"

Callum didn't understand.

"Your promise to me?"

He nodded through his tears, still unable to open his eyes. He'd tried to take care of himself, tried to keep living.

"Cal, please... look at me."

Slowly, Callum opened his eyes. Evan's face was there, fluid and semi-transparent but smiling with all the love in the world.

"Cal," Evan said, and his voice was full of pride and tenderness.

Callum bit his lip, half-smiling, half in tears, and nodded.

"I love you, Cal. I always will."

"I love you too, Evan," Callum managed through his tears. "I never stopped."

Evan's smile brightened. "Good boy."

Callum sputtered a laugh. How could this vision—whatever his brain was conjuring—be so perfectly, essentially Evan?

"Cal, I'm around, okay?"

Callum nodded like a child who refused to accept his dog had died but knew the truth anyway.

"I'm around. In James's laughter. In Anders's kindness. In the family you're building. In every person you help find their way home." Evan's image began to fade. "I'm not gone, Cal. I just changed."

The light dimmed gradually, warmly, until only the soft glow of the Christmas tree remained.

"Callum? Callum?"

James was gently shaking his arm, trying for the fourth time to wake him. "He must have fallen asleep on the sofa," he said to Anders. "Should we wake him?"

They'd both awakened in each other's arms upstairs—a first for both of them—and decided to come down early to make breakfast, hoping to do better than their Christmas morning disaster.

Callum finally stirred, groggy and disoriented. For a moment he wasn't sure where he was, what was real.

"Callum? Everything okay?" James asked, concerned.

Callum rubbed his eyes, flexed his legs. He knew it had been a dream. Of course it had been a dream.

"Yes," he said softly. "Yes, everything is okay."

But clutched against his chest, held carefully in his lap, sat Evan's angel. Her porcelain face was serene in the morning light, and her presence felt like a benediction, a promise kept.

James and Anders exchanged glances, then settled on either side of Callum on the sofa, not asking questions, just offering their quiet presence.

"He's still here, isn't he?" James said quietly, understanding without explanation.

Callum looked at the angel in his hands, then at these two young men who had become his family, who carried forward all the love Evan had taught him to give.

"Yes," he whispered. "He's still here."

Outside, the snow had stopped falling, and the morning sun cast long golden rays through the parlor windows. The Christmas tree lights twinkled softly, the angel kept her eternal watch, and three souls who had found each other in the darkness sat together in the light, understanding finally that love never truly dies—it simply finds new ways to bloom.

In that moment, in that house where Evan had once spoke of Christmas trees and family gatherings, his dreams lived on in the hearts of those who remained, transformed but undiminished, eternal as the love that had created them.

And the angel smiled her porcelain smile.

About the Author

Michael Manosca first pursued a career in the arts, studying in Chicago, but storytelling has always been at the heart of his creative expression. His travels across the world have shaped his perspective, infusing his writing with the depth and nuance of the people and cultures he has encountered.

He explores the intricacies of friendship, the search for identity, and the quiet moments that define us. Through vivid characters and emotional depth, he hopes to craft stories that linger in readers' minds long after the final page.

When not writing, he can be found wandering the northern woods, exploring new cities, or enjoying a lively conversation in a tucked-away café. He currently resides along the western coast of the United States and is already working on his next story.

Also by Michael Manosca

Beyond Ties that Bind

Treffen

Prism

Bloodlines

Almost Always

Reflections at the Window

A Language of Water

www.ingramcontent.com/pod-product-compliance
Lightning Source LLC
Chambersburg PA
CBHW022101170626
46808CB00002B/534